Point Judith

Judy Prescott Marshall

ALSO BY
JUDY PRESCOTT MARSHALL

BE STRONG ENOUGH SERIES
STILL CRAZY
THE INN IN RHODE ISLAND
THE COTTAGE AT THE INN IN RHODE ISLAND

SPIN OFF SERIES
SWEET BLESSINGS

POINT JUDITH

Book One

Lighthouse Series

JUDY PRESCOTT MARSHALL

David Wayne

This one is for you ~ my love!

Cast of Characters

David Wayne ~ Self-made billionaire

Emily Marshall ~ David's aunt and celebrity chef

Grace ~ Real Estate agent

Ella ~ Grace's best friend and boutique owner

Ava ~ Grace's best friend and boutique owner

Geraldine Prescott ~ Investor

Henry ~ Gatehouse keeper

Jimmy ~ Bartender

Dr. Hudson Harbor ~ Grace's fiancé

Bill McGhee ~ Captain of the Bill Pay

Cory James ~ First mate

Red ~ Homeless man

Dr. Danny Ferris ~ David's neighbor

Dr. Stefanie Hong ~ Hudson Harbor's sister

"If we didn't have the storms … we wouldn't be able to enjoy the waves."

POINT JUDITH

Chapter One

David couldn't believe it. He blinked twice, thinking he read the article wrong. He didn't want it to be true. His heart ached as he closed his laptop. "How long have I been gone?"

The woman sitting on the airplane next to him turned toward him and asked, "Are you okay?"

David nodded his head and closed his eyes remembering all the good times he had at the inn. Living in Point Judith was incredible. He got to go fishing every day, swim in the ocean and in the pool at The Dutch Inn. Growing up, he wanted to live in a lighthouse. As he got older, he would dream about being the captain of his own fishing vessel.

David Wayne is a graduate of Princeton University and Caltech. He performed some astonishing feats in the five years after graduating. One day, he was faced with a problem and based on his approach to life—work hard and play hard mentality he developed the perfect solution. After walking into his bank and asking if they could pay his bills for him directly out of his account only to hear his old college roommate, now bank president laugh at him, two months later, David created the software, handed it to his friend and within a year every bank on the West coast was online with the program. By the second year he was a millionaire. From Hong Kong to England to the shores of Bali, international banking everywhere welcomed his approach. David traveled the globe sharing his idea. Today, at the age of thirty-two he is worth more than eight billion dollars. Unlike a lot of his friends, he does not enjoy the bar scene or going away on long all male weekends. He's a homebody. On cool fall days you can find him at his family beach house in Narragansett. He enjoys jogging on the beach prior to sun up, reading the latest John Grisham novel and cooking his own creations. David also likes spending time at his cabin, hunting, fishing, and grilling steaks—prime rib and filet mignon are his favorites. After traveling the world sharing his idea about online bill pay, David was ready to be back home and attend his friend's wedding. His plan was to get settled in at his cabin, build himself an outdoor kitchen and relax on the front porch while enjoying a little solitude, until he read the article about The Lighthouse Inn being torn down.

As soon as the airplane landed David called a buddy of his to see just how bad the inn was.

"Yeah, the bastard just up and left. I'm not going to lie to you, it's a mess, more like a disaster," his friend said before hanging up the phone.

David had the Uber driver drive down Sand Hill Cove. "Stop!" he shouted, opened the car door, got out and nearly dropped to his knees. He stood there looking at the fence, broken sign and unattended landscape. It broke his heart seeing the place left in that condition. David thought about walking to the beach house, but he needed something to take his mind off the inn. He needed time to think and figure out a game plan. He got back in the car and told the driver to take him to the cabin. Forty-five minutes later, the vehicle drove past the gate house and up to David's cabin. The driver opened the trunk, took David's luggage out and asked, "Is that a real cannon?"

"Yes," David replied and handed him a tip. "Thanks, I can take them from here." David reached for his luggage, went inside and opened his laptop. He searched as far back as he could for The Lighthouse Inn trying to see when the inn closed. Then he read a newspaper article claiming the inn shut down in 2017. He called another friend of his that worked at the town hall. He told David he would meet with him next Friday. "Friday?" David started to say, but thanked him for agreeing to see him. "Thanks, I'll see you next week."

The next morning, he wrote down the measurements for each of the appliances, designed the fireplace, and ordered all of the building material. As soon as it was delivered, he got to work, built the framework for the cabinetry and then he constructed the structure. He created a fifty-by-fifty-foot open room for cooking, entertaining and streaming movies.

When all of the construction was complete, he called upon his favorite aunt to help him pick out the outdoor furniture.

She answered the phone on the first ring. "Is this my favorite traveling nephew?"

"Yes, it is," he replied. "I missed you. How are you?"

She laughed. "You missed my cooking. How was Hong Kong?"

"Just as you described," he said into the phone as he reached for his spinach power shake. "By any chance do you want to help me pick out some patio furniture this week?"

"I can go today, if you'd like. I want to see you."

"I'll pick you up at ten," he said and hung up the phone.

They both agreed the sixty-five-inch flat screen TV had to go directly over the stone fireplace. "Oh, David this is fabulous," Aunt Emily declared.

David put his arm around her shoulder and thanked her for helping him. "Are you hungry?"

She smiled from ear to ear. "Starving," she replied and collapsed into a chair knowing David wanted to show off his new grill.

"Good, you rest and I will cook for you for a change."

Working as a chef, Aunt Emily is always on her feet. Besides, no one knows David better than his aunt. She knew he had the entire menu planned out before he picked up the phone this morning and asked for her help.

David headed for the cabin, but turned around and asked, "Aunt Emily, wine or beer?"

"Grab me a cold beer, please." She reached for her cellphone before adding, "When you come out."

Together they grilled an array of fresh vegetables, swordfish and romaine lettuce brushed with olive oil, garlic and thyme. By the time dinner was done they had each consumed three beers. "That was so good," David said as he sat back in his chair. "I never would have thought to add the thyme."

Emily placed her napkin on the table and said she wanted to make homemade ice cream for dessert. "Do you have any frozen fruit?"

"I have a bag of frozen peaches in the pantry freezer," he told her.

"Great, it will only take a short while," she said as she reached for his empty plate.

"I'll clear the table and clean the grill while you whip up the ice cream," he said. "As long as we can sit outside and eat it."

Aunt Emily turned to face him before requesting he stoke up the fire. "Fine with me, but can you put a few more logs on the fire please?"

After they finished their ice cream, they went inside to read. David picked up the newspaper and read aloud the news on The Lighthouse Inn. "I can't believe the town let the place get this bad. It makes me sick."

Aunt Emily agreed with him. "The town should be ashamed of themselves."

David knew she rarely traveled from Watch Hill to Point Judith because she had her own paradise. He also knew Aunt

Emily was busy with her cooking show, blog, traveling to New York every week and she maintained a full social calendar. But, as soon as he returned to Point Judith the first thing he did was drive down Sand Hill Cove.

"Are you okay?" Aunt Emily touched his shoulder. "David," she called out again.

David shook his head. "I'm sorry. Did you say something?"

She gave him a wry grin. "I wish I knew how much the inn meant to you. I should have called you."

He ran his hands through his hair remembering all the great times he had at the establishment. "I remember my father telling me it was time I learned how to swim. He didn't want me to be like my mother––afraid of the water. I learned to swim in that pool. The fishermen taught me what size lure to use when fishing for trout, and what size I needed to use when I went ocean fishing. I grew up in that place. I had my first kiss in the gym, my first taste of blackened catfish in the restaurant and it was the only pool I was allowed to swim in." He sat back in his chair, kicked out his feet and inhaled. "I have to save it."

Chapter Two

The Lighthouse Inn in Rhode Island was originally built in nineteen-sixty-seven as a two-story motor hotel. Back then, they called it The Dutch Inn. The inn offered room and maid service, complimentary breakfast, three restaurants, a gym and an indoor swimming pool. Its location was perfect for anyone wishing to travel from Point Judith to Block Island. Situated in the middle of the block patrons could walk to shops, beaches and the best restaurants in the state. Even the ferry was conveniently located across the street from the inn. Locals would buy day passes to use the inn's swimming pool, dine at the restaurants and invite their families and friends to stay at the inn during special occasions. Fishing captains of the Seven B's, Frances Fleet, Misty Charters, Snappa Charters, Twenty/Aught Sport Fishing and Pamela May Charters to name a few relied on the inn for their casters after a long day or night of fishing. So why is this fabulous establishment in despair? Perhaps bad management? One has to ask how can a once profitable two-hundred-room inn serving fisherman from all over the world be turned over to the wolves for destruction. Rumor has it the lessee is in negotiations with one developer to replace the establishment with a massive parking lot.

The Independent has reported demolition of the Lighthouse Inn building for redevelopment of the land it sits on, will now have to wait until after the state completes a hazardous materials study. The Department of Environmental Management announced what started out as the Dutch Inn and now The Lighthouse Inn is hitting pause on the activities regarding the former hotel, until it can hire a contractor to perform the hazardous building materials assessment.

A month after David got home, a reporter wrote, David Wayne, a native to Point Judith feels strongly about the inn's property being turned into a parking lot. Quoting him as saying, "It's just wrong," David told the Narragansett Times after learning about one developer's plan. "Reconstruction is the only viable alternative to demolition."

Off the record, Mr. Wayne said he was willing to fight for the inn and pay for the entire project himself. "My hope is that the inn will introduce itself and its history to a new generation of anglers to come."

David thought about the inn's location and everything it had to offer.

A different reporter walked up to David and asked if he had any idea what happened to the place.

"Neglect," David said. "There's so much to do and it's all within walking distance," he added. "Think about it. Fishing, golfing, shopping, boating, sailing, horseback riding right down the road, scuba diving, water skiing and in the winter, people can ski at Yawgoo Valley."

"I hear you," the reporter said. "But, look at the place. It would take a miracle to bring that joint back to life."

David considered what he was saying and thought, it's a shame the young man didn't get to see the place when it was open. "It was great growing up in there. The inn had a swimming pool, hot tub, pool table, game room, a gym and something you never see anymore, free parking."

"Yeah, it's a disgrace. I mean the place has a lot to offer if you have money." He opened his folder and read his notes aloud. "Mix-use development in a special district site plan. Boutique style hotel on five acres of prime land in the middle of a multi-million-dollar property." He shook his head. "If only we had a few bucks laying around, huh?"

David chuckled to himself. "Hey, can I see what else you have there?"

The reporter handed David his file. "Sure, knock yourself out."

David read aloud, "First floor has twelve thousand square feet, a twenty-two hundred square foot dining room and four meeting rooms." He handed the file back to the young man and told him. "I wish you luck with your article."

Chapter Three

When Emily's sister and brother-in-law died in a tragic auto accident, she became the sole relative to their son, David. He was thirteen at the time, now he is her favorite taste tester.

Emily Marshall is a television celebrity chef. She has seven cookbooks, a food blog with over ninety-thousand subscribers and on her Instagram page she has four-million followers. Her gardens featuring her own hand-selected veggies, herbs, shrubs and flower beds have been featured in Garden Gate, Better Homes and Gardens, Country Living and House and Garden magazines. Her property boasts the only barn on Watch Hill. It is also home to her studio where she films her weekly television episodes. The internet famous chef has a stunning home on the property surrounded by architectural flower pots filled with flowering trees such as wisteria, dogwood, limelight hydrangea, and viburnum. Her cutting gardens are located on the sunny side of the property. Follow the two rows of blue hydrangeas to the end and you will find anemone, deep purple hydrangea, Asiatic lily, poppy, peony, sea holly, phlox, zinnia, snapdragon, dahlia, foxglove, coneflower, cosmos, and her favorite David Austin roses.

Every recipe she creates features her own fresh herbs. She follows a Mediterranean diet that emphasizes on plant-based foods and healthy fats. A few years ago, she planted fruit trees next to her Victorian style iron and glass solarium where she keeps her olive, lemon, and lime trees. Behind her seven-thousand-square-foot home overlooking the Atlantic is a stone patio where she hosts many parties, soirees and meetings. Besides her favorite nephew, seeing her calendar full makes her happy. She's a socialite, attends fancy parties, dines at expensive restaurants and hangs out with famous people.

Friday mornings, Emily travels to the small town of Millbrook, New York to meet with her producer and general manager. She uses the nearly three-hour drive to and from to write her blog, create new recipes and explore her inner self. On occasion she will ask her driver to stop along the road so she can hand out samples of her latest dish to truckers parked at rest areas. She has yet to find one who has not enjoyed her samplings. If a truck driver likes her sample, she is happy and she knows she has a hit on her hands.

Often, she will stay for the weekend, visit the local farmer's markets, and stop in for a bite to eat at the Millbrook Cafe or Charlotte's Restaurant in the heart of horse country. She's well aware they know who she is, because they always give her the best tables, service and complimentary glass of whatever she is drinking. Her driver never seems to mind the long stay. He too has a taste for fine dining and back country roads. David introduced the two right after they graduated from high school. In fact, the six-foot-two linebacker is so close to her, he calls her Aunt Emily. Emily refers to him as her favorite adopted son from another mother. The two are inseparable. A neighbor mistakenly referred to them as lovers. Another time, someone asked if he lived with her. Aunt Emily laughed aloud and told them to mind their own damn business. Declaring they should be ashamed of themselves. In all honesty, she loved him almost as much as she did her nephew. She was a respectable lady; he was simply her driver. It was not her place to announce his sexual preferences. If he enjoyed the company of another man...than so be it.

Chapter Four

February 14 is a day to celebrate love. Married or not. The ladies were headed to a well-known hot spot for cocktails and dinner followed by dancing in the back room at ten. The Stonebridge Restaurant served the best crab cakes in Milford and the ladies loved the vibe, especially at the bar. Ava, Ella and Grace each had less than a year to go before they all turned thirty. Ava and Ella owned a successful boutique in Stratford. Ever since they were in the tenth grade the two women have dreamed of owning a business together. Ava is definitely the fashionista of the two. She loves fabrics rich in texture. She's a trend setter, a master at mixing and matching various textiles. Ella has the head for business. She is a genius when it comes to budgets, spreadsheets and saving money. If you visit any town along the waterways in Connecticut, you paid a visit to The Beach Boutique on Birdseye Street.

Grace on the other hand was at a crossroad, working in real estate meant working a lot of hours, nearly seven days a week. She started working in the business straight out of high school. In coastal Connecticut, the market was always hot. The towns are charming and they offer over three-hundred miles of shoreline. The scenery is so gorgeous, she did not mind driving clients around. By the time she was twenty-five she had landed her first big client, Geraldine Prescott. Miss Prescott was big money. She bought large estates that were in need of improving or renovating. Grace worked with a lot of entrepreneurs before, but no one turned a profit like Miss Prescott and, she was very generous with her commissions. If Grace got the price down to what Miss Prescott was willing to pay, she rewarded Grace with expensive perks, items Grace would never think of purchasing for herself. Gucci, Prada, and Louis Vuitton to name a few. Prescott's last purchase was a four-million-dollar estate in Greenwich. Grace earned one hundred and twenty-thousand dollars on that transaction. Her reward for finding the gem—a new pair of Jimmy Choo heels and matching handbag worth forty-nine-hundred dollars. Miss Prescott told her she chose the leopard print so Grace could wear them with blue jeans, or a little black dress. There was one problem with Grace's lifestyle. It left her very little time to find Mr. Right and her biological clock was ticking. As much as she loved working in the business, meeting new people and making good money, she was ready to settle down. She wanted a family of her own.

Grace was in her car when her cell phone rang. She looked over and read, "Ella!" Tapped the accept button and said, "Hi."

"Hey girl! Are you ready for tonight?" Ella asked.

"Oh, hell yeah!" Grace replied as she turned into her driveway and picked up her cellphone. "I just got home, wait until you see what I'm wearing."

"Great, we wanted to make sure you didn't have to work late...again."

"Stop, I'll order our cocktails and meet you at the bar by eight. Love you both, heading for the shower. Ciao Bella." Grace was never late. Unlike Ella and Ava, she did not have a partner to greet her clients. She had to be on time or they found a new realtor.

Grace took one last look at herself in the tall mirror. "If this dress doesn't find me a man, I'm giving up." The Sheen Bae draped front halter neck backless dress was a killer. Short, sexy and the drawstring at the neck left little to the imagination.

Grace walked in and all heads turned her way. As soon as the bartender spotted her, he waved with his hand and pointed toward the end of the bar—their usual seats. Three stools near the entrance to the restaurant. Jimmy held up three fingers and Grace nodded. She watched him pour her a dirty martini, Ella's Malibu Bay Breeze and Ava's Manhattan.

Grace could not help overhearing the four men sitting in the corner booth behind her. They were laughing and congratulating someone's promotion.

"The rest of your trio has arrived," Jimmy said to her as he set their cocktails down. He nodded to Ella and Ava adding, "Ladies. Enjoy." Jimmy was the perfect bartender. He remembered everyone's drink choice, delivered them on time and he never let anyone drive home drunk. He literally had a line of Uber drivers at his beck and call. Best of all, he watched out for the single ladies. He protected them from cads. He was also happily married with three adorable little boys and a girl on the way.

Grace stood up to hug Ella and Ava.

"Look at you. Love the dress," Ava said as she set her bag on the bar.

Grace kissed her on the cheek. "I bought it at your boutique."

Ella kissed Grace hello and pointed to her feet. "Are those?"

Grace lifted her foot and both Ella and Ava looked at the soul. "Oh, my goodness!" They both responded.

"I'm not even going to ask how much," Ella said and took her seat.

"Stop, I would never spend this much on a pair of shoes, even if it did come with a matching handbag."

Ava sat down on the other side of Grace and whispered in her ear, "Don't turn around, but the redhead just said he hopes you're not married."

Grace spun around and looked directly at the group of men. Only one man was wearing a wedding band. When she made eye contact with the redhead, he raised his glass and smiled at her. She smiled at him and nodded gracefully his way before turning back around.

Ava raised her glass and said, "Happy Valentine's Day!"

Ella lifted hers and replied, "To finding true love, making our first million and to Jimmy—the best damn bartender in the world."

After the first round of drinks, Jimmy told the ladies their table was ready.

"So, Jimmy, I heard you and Mrs. Yeno are expecting another baby," Ava said before turning to leave.

Grace tugged on her arm. "You had your chance. Now give it up."

"Seriously, Ava!" Ella pushed her from behind. "Are you going to ask him every time he has a child?"

"I wish I was pregnant," Grace said as they reached their table. "I'm not getting any younger, I better freeze my eggs."

They laughed at the thought of Grace feeling so old she wanted to freeze her eggs. "Stop making fun of me," she said. Adding, "I want to have children. Besides, I already made the appointment at the HRC Fertility Clinic."

"Wow, you are serious," Ella said and asked for another Malibu.

Before Grace sat down, she told them she was not waiting any longer. "I want to have children while I am still young."

Ella sat to her right and Ava took her seat on the other side of Grace. Before their server came back to the table Ava told Grace. "He's out there waiting for you. I am sure of it."

They did not need to look at the menu. Ella ordered the crispy calamari for everyone to share and the Blackened Ahi tuna for herself. Grace and Ava ordered their favorite—the mango salmon.

Everyone paid for their share of the bill, ordered another round of drinks and took them out to the back deck for an evening of live music and dancing. First song had them all on the dance floor. "Flowers" by Miley Cyrus a sultry slow groove allowing the ladies to own the dance floor. Ella was smooth, gracious and limber as she danced circles around Grace and Ava. Ella was different on the dance floor, relaxed with not a care in the world. But in the store, she was the money manager worried all the time. Ella feared not having enough money to pay for their dream, but at the end of the day, the two women always showed a substantial profit.

Grace turned around before the song ended and saw the redhead standing next to one of the other men from his table leaning up against the wall. The two men looked as if they were eager to hit the dance floor. Hips swaying, heads moving with the music. Grace used her index finger to call them onto the dance floor and before she knew it five songs later, she was slow dancing to "Thinking Out Loud."

When the song ended, Grace looked into his eyes and said, "My name is Grace."

He smiled at her. Lifted her hand to his lips, kissed her finger tips and replied, "I am delighted to meet you, Grace. I'm Hudson. May I buy you a drink?"

Grace's insides surged as he held her hand. She did not want to move. She wanted to stay right there on the dance floor with his arms wrapped tightly around her. She took back her hand and replied, "I would like that." Smiling, she said, "Thank you for the dance."

Grace and Hudson sat at the table with his friend, Melvin, along with Ava and Ella. Grace smiled as she introduced him. "Ava, Ella, this is Hudson."

Melvin stood and shook Grace's hand. "I'm Melvin, it's nice to meet you."

"It's a pleasure," she replied and sat down.

The waiter brought over a round of drinks just as Melvin announced they had to leave soon because he had an early meeting. When he said that Grace's heart stopped beating. She did not want the evening to end. Hudson tapped her on her arm and asked if he could give her his number. She blushed seeing Ava and Ella's reaction. "Of course," she replied and handed him her business card as she accepted the napkin with Hudson's number written on it.

Chapter Five

The Lighthouse Inn was in the news again. Located across from the Block Island Ferry, the Lighthouse Inn of Galilee was a fun, casual beach hotel situated in the authentic fishing village of Galilee, Rhode Island. It was the perfect location to relax and enjoy southern Rhode Island. Once again, the state's decision not to accept any of the proposals to redevelop the former Lighthouse Inn left officials and residents blindsided. The Department of Environmental Management said it plans to allow two of the three lots on the five-acre parcel to remain as parking and tear down the defunct hotel on the third. The DEM called the move "a way forward" to make the property more attractive to prospective investors. There was only one problem. Who would buy the property? What were their intentions? If they tear it down and do not replace the hotel, where does that leave the anglers? Especially the men and women returning in the early morning hours hoping to get a little sleep before heading back out onto the water or even home?

David knew he had to act fast. Town officials could pull a fast one at any moment. He called a buddy of his working for the Department of Conservation to see if he knew anyone on the planning board. "I need to get a detailed list of what they are looking for," he said.

"Let me see when the next town meeting is scheduled for and I will get back to you."

David hung up the phone and called a woman he dated a few years ago to see if she heard anything.

"Savannah, it's David Wayne. How have you been?"

"Good, well if you call being a single mom to four boys good."

"I'm sorry to hear that. I didn't know."

"It's fine. I kicked his ass out two years ago. I'm better off without him. We all are. In fact, he moved to Tennessee so I don't have to deal with the bullshit of who gets the boys on the weekends and holidays. How are you? I heard you made a lot of money on a hunch."

David laughed. "Yeah, you could say that. I'm doing well. I have a question for you. What do you know about the old Lighthouse Inn?"

Savannah worked in the county clerk's office. She knew everyone and she wasn't shy about letting you know it. "I heard they want to tear it down. Town officials are not happy the way he left the place. I mean who the hell renovates a place just to walk away?"

"Any word on what the county is hoping will happen with the building?"

She laughed. "Yeah, a miracle so they can start receiving revenue from the place. The only thing the county cares about is making money. They want their taxes paid."

"Are there back taxes owed?" he asked and grabbed a piece of paper and a pen.

"Let me look. Hang on. Actually, let me call you back. I may have something worth sharing with you."

"You're the best!" He said and hung up the phone.

A half hour later, Savannah called David back and told him someone paid all the back taxes. "Apparently, someone has a hidden agenda. The guy holding the lease on the property paid the taxes in full, but between you and me he didn't pay them with his own money. He has a backer."

"I owe you dinner," he said.

"Send me flowers and sign the card. It will drive everyone in the office crazy."

David laughed out loud. "You always were a lot of fun. Sunflowers, right?"

"Oh yeah, you need anything else call me. Take care, Mr. Wayne."

David laughed again knowing she was busting someone's ass when she said his name aloud.

Chapter Six

Grace walked into the house, left her business card on the counter next to the sign-in sheet and began taking notes. The first thing she noticed was the house was immaculate, practically brand new and it even smelled of fresh paint. The fireplace was gorgeous, big round rocks in shades of pale pink, tan and mossy green. She smiled when she saw the twinkling lights wrapped around the wood in the fire place. Of course, she had to flip the switch to see the glow. Straight out of a magazine. The first floor offered a nice size kitchen, dining room and a formal living room. Upstairs were four bedrooms and two bathrooms. All of the rooms were painted in a pale yellow, even the bathrooms. She entered the last bedroom at the end of the hall and saw a man sitting in an accent chair with a shot gun lying across his lap. She asked him if he was okay. He just looked at her. Any other woman would have screamed, but Grace stood her ground. She told him her name and that she was the listing agent for the house. Then she asked him if he needed help. He raised one hand to his chin and told her she needed to leave. She took one deep breath and responded by telling him her business card was on the counter, adding if you would like to talk to someone, I am a great listener and I know how to keep a secret. After he nodded, she turned to leave, but stopped in the doorway for a moment longer. Long enough for him to take his other hand off the gun stock. "I don't care what time it is. Call me," she said to him and left. When she got to her car, she glanced up at the bedroom window and noticed he was standing behind the sheer looking down at her. She prayed he would be okay.

Lunchtime, Gracie received a call from Hudson thanking her for the dance and asked if they could meet on Thursday for lunch at Founders House. "Whatever time works for you," he said.

She glanced down at her calendar and told him two o'clock worked for her.

Grace spent the rest of her day reorganizing her schedule. She told one couple she had a family emergency one weekend and another person she just flat out told them she could not work that weekend. As tempting as it was, she did not call Ella or Ava. She wanted to see how things played out with Hudson before getting her hopes up. She thought about calling the clinic, but ignored the urge to cancel.

Ten o'clock that night her cellphone rang. It was from an unidentified number. She set the book down and answered the call anyway. "Hello."

"Hey, it's Steve. I'm sorry about today," he said and she knew it was the homeowner.

"Are you okay?"

"I'm better," he replied adding, "I hope I didn't frighten you too much."

"I don't scare easily." She cracked a smile. "I'm glad you called."

"I was expecting a man to show up."

"A man?"

"My wife said she was sending over her agent."

"Umm, did you intend on shooting him?"

Silence

"Well, then I am glad God put me in your path and not one of my male coworkers," Grace said into the phone.

There was a slight pause before he responded, "I would not have shot him. I was just trying to scare him."

She took a deep breath. "I assure you both of the men in my office are happily married. Why do you...?"

"My daughter told me my wife was dating a man who wore a suit and tie every day."

"Yeah, it is definitely not one of the two men who work in my office, they wear khakis and a button-down shirt if you're lucky."

"I heard you are going to list the house for over nine-hundred-thousand dollars."

"It is worth every penny."

"Thank you, I built it. My son and daughter said they want to live with me full time."

She thought for a minute. "Do you want me to take the house off the market?"

"No," he said abruptly. "I hate the design. I built the damn thing for her. I do not want to stay there another day."

Grace nodded in agreement, thinking about how painful it had to be for him. Then she chuckled thinking about the poor design, absolutely lifeless. Nothing about it said a happy family lived there. It was more a gallery than a home.

"Can I buy you a cup of coffee?" he said. "I feel bad for what I did."

"Hmm, let me ponder your question for a minute. No, you owe me dinner. Besides, I have an appointment at nine with a couple that I am sure will take up most of my day. I'll meet you at the Stonebridge Restaurant at six if that works for you."

"I'll be there," he said and the call ended.

The next day, Grace met with three clients, listed a parcel of raw land for two-million dollars and totally forgot to eat.

As soon as she finished with her last appointment she headed over to the restaurant. Sat in her usual seat, ordered an appetizer, sipped her cocktail and texted Ella. Grace asked if she heard from Melvin. Before he left, he handed Ella his business card, kissed her on the cheek and told her he would see her soon.

Ella typed, "Yes, we're going to dinner on Saturday, but I'm not sure about this one."

"Why do you say that?"

"He works all the damn time! Hey, I have to go. I just set the alarm. Closing up the store. Call me later."

"Bye."

She was still sitting at the bar talking to Jack about Ella and Ava expanding a new clothing line at their boutique, when Steve walked in. She waved to him and asked him what he wanted to drink.

"I will have a scotch on the rocks." Then he sat down next her and handed her an envelope. "You can open it later," he said and set a fifty-dollar bill on the bar.

She smiled at him trying to figure him out. "Are feeling better tonight?"

He snickered.

She chuckled before asking, "Is there anything you like about your house?"

"There is no place or room for me and the kids. Every room is hers. What's to like?"

Grace snapped her neck. "Really?"

"I'm a contractor. I own tools. I thought about building a garage for all my stuff, but she didn't even give me a spot to hang a fishing pole. She even told the kids to have a yard sale and sell their old toys."

Grace lifted her martini and drank it entirely. "Jack, we will be back for dinner in an hour." Then she turned to Steve and said, "Come on, drink up. I have something I want to show you."

They walked over to her car and she drove to a house she had just put on the market. It had a huge four bay garage and a barn big enough for any man to call his own. As soon as she pulled up to the house, he loved it. It was a one-story ranch. "Follow me, I have to show you the finished basement," she said to him and led the way.

When he saw the game room, gym, full bathroom and the storage room big enough for all the kids gear he turned to her and asked, "How much?"

She held up one finger and said, "Wait. I have one more surprise to show you." They went back upstairs and when she turned on the flood light, opened the patio door and pointed to the backyard, he gasped.

"I have to show my kids this house."

"The previous owner used to work for a tree house company. He had twins, a boy and a girl. The inside has two separate areas." The tree house was about twelve feet above the shade garden. She reached for his elbow and brought him out onto the back deck. To his right was an in-ground pool and a basketball court. The pool was surrounded by tall grasses and an arbor for relaxing after a long day at work.

Steve stood there shaking his head. When he pointed up and said, "Thank you."

She knew she was sent to his house for a reason. "The asking price is seven hundred and fifty."

"I'll take it!"

She closed the door, locked it and turned off the lights. "I'm starving and you owe me dinner."

Chapter Seven

David met with his aunt Emily at her home to discuss his thoughts on the old Lighthouse Inn being demolished. "I have a meeting with the town board next Friday to discuss my plans," he said.

"David, I understand your love for the inn," she replied as she poured him a glass of her famous pomegranate spritzer. "I have to ask; how much money are you willing to invest to save the inn?" She sat down next to him and slid a dessert plate filled with crinkled chocolate chip cookies in front of him. She knew he had enough of his own money to invest in the project, however she never turned her back on him. She waited for him to finish chewing before letting him know she wanted in on the deal. "I'll invest whatever amount of money you need as long as you name it after me." She laughed aloud before adding, "I'm kidding about the name. Seriously, let me know how much and I will cut you a check. By any chance, do you know what it will entail to get the place up and running?"

He shook his head. "I need to wait for all the reports to come back from waste management and hazmat." He took a sip of his juice and smiled. "The report is over eight-hundred pages long."

"What?" She declared and slapped her hand on the table. "What could possibly be in it?"

"Well, to start it has the site preparation, excavation plan, structural engineering, electrical engineering, archaeological and biological resources, utilities, and that is just the beginning." He looked at her with the intent of a man on a mission. "I am not going to sit still and let them tear down that inn. Aunt Emily, the fishing industry depends on that establishment."

She nodded approvingly. "Let me know how I can help." She smiled at him. "I'll host a fundraiser."

Raising money for various organizations in Rhode Island was another one of her specialties. In the past, she has raised millions of dollars for local charities. "I am serious about investing," she said and took a deep breath before adding, "I am very proud of you."

He laughed knowing she would say those exact words. "I can pay for the project on my own, but if you would like to be an investor and share in the profit that would be great and thank you." He kissed her cheek. "Your approval means a lot to me."

They spoke about his plans to move the swimming pool to a new location. "After I watched the video on YouTube, I was devastated," he said. "Aunt Emily, I have to do something.

Besides, I have traveled long enough." He leaned over and gave her another kiss on the cheek. "I have missed you so much."

"I missed you more than you can imagine," she replied and then asked, "what are your plans for this weekend?" Hoping they could have dinner and talk about all the places he traveled to.

He tossed his hand in the air. "I am hosting a bachelor party for Dale and a few of his friends at the beach house."

"Sounds like fun." She stood up and grabbed the pitcher to refill his glass, adding, "I can't believe he's getting married. All I can say is she must be an angel."

David laughed. "Yeah, Friday should be a blast. First, I have to go to the town hall, then I have to stop by Ferry Wharf Fish Market on my way home and pick up the food for the New England clambake."

"Nice, you always did love clambakes. How about I send over a nice dessert?"

"Perfect," he replied. "You know the only thing I'm good at is making ice cream." David kissed her on the cheek and told her to have a nice day. She made him promise her he would keep her posted on the plan to save the inn.

Chapter Eight

Friday afternoon, Hudson called Grace and asked if he could take her out for dinner and a movie. "I had a great time the other day. I was thinking we could get together again."

"Tonight?" She replied.

"Tonight, or tomorrow night," he said adding, "whatever night is good for you. I would like to take you to my favorite restaurant to see if you approve."

"I can meet you tonight at seven if that works for you."

"Great, I'll meet you at Gabriel's of Westport, 27 Powers Court." Hudson went to hang up the phone, but instead told her how delighted he was to be seeing her again. "Grace, I'm glad you accepted my hand and danced with me. I am excited to see you again."

Her heart skipped a beat. "I can still smell your cologne, Creed. Am I correct?"

He laughed. "Yes, but I did not buy it for myself. My sister buys it for me every year for my birthday. I have others if you care to take a whiff. My patients are constantly trying to get me to smell attractive for some reason."

"Your sister has good taste. I like the way you smell."

Once again, he laughed. "I was so captivated by your appearance. I can't remember if you were wearing any perfume or not. I guess I will just have to get a little closer to find out."

"I better step up my game. Umm, let's see if you can guess what I will be wearing." She looked at the phone. "Wait. Did you say your patients?"

"Yes, I have a family practice here in Westport. The older women are constantly trying to get me hitched. You know daughters, nieces, neighbors. Hence the twenty bottles of cologne in my cabinet. I look forward to seeing you, goodbye."

Grace could hear someone in the background asking if he was ready to see his next patient.

Grace hung up the phone, took a deep breath and immediately called Ava and Ella. "So, Hudson is..."

"A doctor," Ella said. "We know Melvin told me last night. So, did he call you? Are you going out with him?"

Grace sat in the recliner, kicked up her legs and answered with a big smile on her face. "I'm meeting him at Gabriele's tonight."

They both shouted in the phone, "Nice restaurant!"

"What are you wearing?" Ava asked as she looked around the store trying to find something sexy and yet elegant for Grace to wear on a date with a doctor.

Grace thought for a moment and then remembered the black Lascana tie at the shoulder jumpsuit Ava picked out for her last week. "The jumpsuit you made me buy," she replied and Ava agreed it was perfect for her first date.

"Second date, we ate lunch the other day," Grace replied before attempting to hang up the phone.

"Wait, call us and let us know how it went," Ella said.

Grace was so nervous; she was ten minutes late. Hudson stood the moment he saw her enter the restaurant. He was not only charming, pulchritudinous and smart he was captivating in such a way, Grace could not take her eyes off him. She leaned in and kissed his cheek telling him how sorry she was for being late.

"You are so worth it," he said and pulled her chair out from the table.

Grace sat down and inhaled before telling him he was wearing a new cologne. "You're wearing Polo." She smiled. "It smells amazing on you. Umm, would you like to guess what I am wearing?"

Hudson grinned from ear to ear, stood closer, held his hand out to her and hugged her tight before telling her. "Beautiful by Estée Lauder," he replied and kissed her on the lips before whispering in her ear. "I bought you something." He leaned down and picked up the pink gift bag from Macy's. Then he handed her the entire collection.

Grace smiled warmly as she gazed at the lotion, perfume, body powder, and bath salts. "This is so sweet." She kissed his lips, long and hard before adding, "Thank you."

"Mmm, I told the woman behind the counter I needed something for my beautiful date and she suggested this. As soon as I smelled it, I thought of you."

The waiter set their menus down and asked if they would like something to drink.

Hudson held his hand out. "Grace?"

"Let's start with a bottle of wine. You choose."

Hudson nodded. "How about a bottle of Chateau La Mission? Grace do you like seafood?"

"Love it!" She replied and set her bag on the floor.

"We'll start with the seafood tower and the caviar on the side."

"Perfect. Would you like the small or large?"

"Large, please." Hudson raised his eyebrows at Grace. "I haven't eaten all day. I was like a schoolboy getting ready for his first prom."

She tapped her hand on his. "I'm glad it wasn't just me. I had butterflies in my stomach all day thinking about you."

Hudson blushed as he lifted his menu.

Grace was salivating when she read hers. "I'm ready to order if you are."

Hudson set his menu down and told Grace to go ahead and place her order. She asked for the pan seared salmon with fingerling potatoes, baby bok choy and ammoglio sauce.

Hudson smiled and said, "I'll have the scallops."

Grace looked down and read cauliflower puree, shaved Brussel sprouts, corn and cherry tomatoes, bacon and citrus gastrique. "I almost ordered that." She raised her eyebrows several times.

The waiter took back the menus and said he would be right back with their bottle of wine and starters.

"The movie starts at ten so we should have plenty of time," Hudson said before reaching over and moving a strand of hair from her face. Then he pointed his finger in the air telling her they had to go to Mrs. London's Bakery & Café on their way to the theater. "Her pastries are the best on the East Coast."

Grace inhaled before telling him decadent desserts are her weakness. "I love Italian pastries."

He smiled warmly at her. "I can't walk by a French bakery without going inside. The owner started in Greenwich Village back in the 1970s, he was a pastry chef, his wife was his apprentice. They always dreamed of opening a bakery together."

"What a beautiful love story," Grace said as the waiter poured their wine.

They enjoyed their dinner and time together so much, they decided to skip the movie and walk to the bakery instead. Afterwards, they sat along the Saugatuck River laughing and making plans to meet for the weekend. Hudson used his napkin to wipe custard from Grace's chin before kissing her. "I have never felt this way about anyone. Do I have to wait another day to see you? I hope I don't frighten you with my words and feelings. Grace, I am falling in love with you."

She thought for a moment. She was twenty-nine. Old enough to know he was everything she had ever wanted. Taking his face in her hands she told him, "I have waited a long time to hear those words. I have to know––this is." She inhaled, leaned back and smiled.

"Is real?" He said. "Grace ..." he started to say something and then remembered his manners. "I am not going anywhere. I promise you."

For the next several weeks, Grace and Hudson were inseparable. From concerts at the Met to the Westport Country Playhouse to jet setting to Bermuda for a surprise weekend getaway to traveling to Wyoming for a friend's wedding. It wasn't until they got back to Hudson's house when Grace decided it was time. Her insides were pulsating. "That was a long flight. Do you mind if I take a quick shower before going home?" She asked.

Hudson told her he would be in his study, reading. A half-hour later, Grace stood in the doorway, wearing a short, pale pink negligee. Her long hair was tied up in a loose bun. Hudson's eyes raised above his book. He gently set it to the side before shaking his head. Grace sauntered over to him, sat on his lap and asked if she could spend the night. First, she shrugged her shoulders, then she smiled warmly at him and said, "I love you so much. I can't imagine spending another day," she winked. "Or night without you."

Hudson let out a deep sigh before passionately kissing her, pulling her closer to him. He stood up and carried her upstairs to the master bedroom, sat her down on the edge of the bed and told her he was going to take quick shower. "Don't start without me," he teased.

She swatted his derrière and pulled down the bedspread before climbing under the covers. When he returned, she pretended to be asleep. Hudson quietly got under the covers, kissed her on the forehead and whispered, "Good night, beautiful."

She giggled until he started tickling her turning her giggles to laughter. Hudson made love to her and when she was satisfied, he told her she made him the happiest man in the world. "I love you so much Grace."

Chapter Nine

Before David knew it, six o'clock had rolled in and his first guest had arrived. He opened the door and shook Randy's hand. "Welcome, it's nice to see you again," he said and then waved to the other guys as they pulled into the driveway. "Great, everyone is on time. Hey, grab yourself something to drink." He pointed to the makeshift bar set up on the back deck.

Randy thanked him and told him the beach house still looked great. "The last time I was here, we had just graduated high school," he called out over his shoulder as he stepped onto the deck. "The view is still incredible," Randy shouted as he gazed at the sun hovering over the Atlantic.

The groom had arrived with two men David had never met before. The bride's brother and a guy he worked with.

"George, Bobby this is my best friend, David."

David stuck his hand out to greet them as they stepped inside. "Nice to meet the two of you. Help yourselves to a cocktail. There's a cooler filled with Michelob Ultra next to the grill and plenty of liquor on the side table." He closed the door and told Dale he wouldn't have missed his wedding for anything. He grabbed him by his shoulders adding, "I can't believe it. You're getting married."

"Huh, I can't believe it either, but here I am. Hey, thanks for coming back on such short notice."

David shook his head. "I was ready to come home. Believe me, traveling around the world for four straight years is not what they put it up to and I am honored to be your best man. Come on, it's time for a toast."

After everyone helped themselves to a cold beer. David held his bottle up and announced, "To Dale and Dawn, may they be blessed with love in abundance, children at their feet and a happy home life." David tapped his beer to Dale's. "Cheers, Buddy."

"Cheers," they all shouted.

David pointed to the smoke down on the beach and asked if everyone was hungry. Next to the fire pit was a small oval table and chairs, six tiki torches and a side table with plates, another cooler and a large gift box. "Shall we move this party to the beach?" David asked as he held the gate open for everyone to go down onto the sand.

Dale was the first person to walk up to the smoke. "Nothing better than a fresh clambake. The pit is incredible."

"Yeah, I put it in about a year ago."

"How does one go about building such a beast?" George asked.

"I started by excavating an eight-by-eight-foot hole, then I filled it with about two tons of fieldstone. This morning, I put nine inches of hardwood in. I like oak, but some people use maple. I dumped eight bags of charcoal in, lit the fire, let it burn for about four hours and then I add a layer of seaweed. Under the plastic tarp is a canvas tarp that I soak in water overnight. I have bags of mussels, clams, corn, potatoes and lobsters," he said as he reached down and started to pull the tarp back.

Dale grabbed the other end to help him. "Man, it smells amazing," Dale said as he started to fold the tarp. "Look at those lobsters."

George stood back in awe. "Hey, why are they all on their backs?"

David laughed. "It keeps them from moving around. Grab a plate and help yourself," he said as he handed Dale the first plate.

Dale took hold of two lobsters before reaching for his corn, potato and bags of clams and mussels.

Everyone took a seat at the table, feasted on their dinner, drank more beer and laughed about Dale finally finding a woman who would put up with his not so funny jokes.

"Can you imagine owning a gorgeous home on the beach and not spending your summers in it?" Dale said as he put his napkin on the table.

"I'm not a big fan of crowds," David announced. "I like being at the cabin, it's cooler and I can go skinny dipping day or night without anyone watching me."

Bobby said he wasn't a big fan of the beach either and then asked where David's cabin was located.

"About forty-five minutes from here," David replied adding, "it's quiet. I can swim, hike, kayak on the lake and read on the front porch in my own silence."

"The cabin is nice," Dale said. "Still, it's a shame a place like this stays empty all summer."

"Huh," George said and then asked to use David's bathroom. Several times David looked up wondering if he ate something that did not settle right with him. More than a half hour had passed before George reappeared. When he came back down to the beach the men had moved to the Adirondack chairs with their beers. George announced he was ready for another cold one. "Does anyone else want a beer?" As he held his bottle up.

"We're good," Dale called out.

David got up and set the box down in front of the groom. "We can't have a celebration without a token to remember it by."

Dale opened the box and could not believe what was inside. David smiled, "Aunt Emily suggested the whiskey," he laughed adding, "the cigars were my idea."

Dale held up five boxes of Gran Habano No.5 cigars before handing each person their own miniature bottle of Midleton

Very Rare Silent Distillery Chapter One Whiskey. He took the first cigar out and smelled it, shaking his head ever so slightly. "Remember graduation day?"

David laughingly replied, "How could I forget it? Aunt Emily handed each of us a cigar and told us successful men and women smoke these."

A few minutes later the men were puffing on their cigars, laughing about the old times and watching a Sea Ray 650 Fly go by.

"That's sweet," George said.

"You should see David's yacht," Randy said before taking another sip from his whiskey.

David told everyone he had been away traveling until he heard the news of The Lighthouse Inn. "I have to try and save the place," he said and grabbed an open bottle of Glendalough 17 pouring just enough to cover the ice in everyone's glass.

Dale asked if David was dating anyone.

David laughed aloud. "Huh, I met a nice woman in France. We dated for a few weeks and then she told me her husband was returning from China. Hey, you should stop up to the cabin some time. I built an outdoor kitchen."

"I can't believe you don't spend the summer here?" George said, looking up at the house.

David raised his shoulders and said, "What can I tell you." Then he asked if anyone wanted a piece of pecan pie.

Dale snapped his neck back. "You have got to try his Aunt Emily's pecan pie. It goes perfectly with whiskey. I can't believe she made my favorite."

It was past ten when everyone left. David cleaned up the beach before heading up to the house. He knew Maria would be in bright and early on Monday to help clean the rest. He rinsed the glasses, put them in the dishwasher and headed to his study to read the proposed site plan one of the town officials had given to him.

Monday morning, he was sitting at the kitchen counter when he heard a knock on the front door. "George, you, okay?" David asked, puzzled as to why he had come back.

"Yeah, I forgot my watch in your bathroom the other night. You mind grabbing it for me?"

"Not at all, come on in." David closed the door and asked him if he wanted a cup of coffee.

"No, thanks. I'm in a bit of a hurry."

When David returned, George was standing in the kitchen. David asked again, "Are you sure you don't want a cup of coffee?"

"No, thanks." George reached out and took hold of his watch and stated he had to get going. "I wasn't sure if you would still be here or not."

David gave him a wry grin. "You take care." He opened the door and watched George get in his Corvette and drive away seconds before Maria pulled into the driveway.

"Good morning, David," she said as she got out of her car. "How did your party go?" She asked as she entered the foyer holding a bag of groceries.

David reached for the bag and told her it went off without a hitch.

"Hahaha," she said. "I always liked Dale. I'm glad *he* found someone to share his life with."

"Okay, that's my cue to get to work."

"I met a very nice young lady at Taylor's the other day. She's pretty and works in finance."

David kissed Maria on the cheek. "Thanks for taking such good care of me. I promise one day, I will find the right woman." He grabbed his coffee and went up to his study to make his notes before heading back over to the town hall.

Maria had been Aunt Emily's house manager before starting to work for David. He was lucky to obtain her services. She works for a select few. Maria takes care of David's cleaning, laundry, inventory, ordering online and grocery shopping. He would be lost without her. She also takes care of his cabin. The only house she does not have to worry about is the gatehouse up at the cabin, Henry lives there and in lieu of rent, he mows the lawn, cleans the pool and makes sure David is never out of firewood. Henry also takes care of all his own needs. Says he doesn't need a woman meddling in his business. He likes living alone, trapping, fishing, and hunting for food.

Chapter Ten

Grace's cellphone rang. As soon as she saw it was Hudson, her heart started beating in her chest. She answered the call on the first ring. "Hello."

"Hello, beautiful. I was wondering if you had time to have dinner with me tonight?"

She picked up her calendar and read five o'clock appointment with the Clarks knowing it would take her at least an hour to show them the house on Kings Way. Of course, they would want to take a stroll down to the beach on her time before deciding to make an offer. "Can we meet at seven? I have a showing at five."

"Perfect," he replied adding, "seven at my house."

"Will you be cooking tonight?"

"I'll have you know; I am a pretty good cook."

"Sounds wonderful. I will text you if I am running late," she said and disconnected the phone.

Grace never ran through a house faster than she did with the Clarks. She was thankful they toured the neighborhood and strolled down the beach prior to their meeting. "We would like to buy the house," Mr. Clark announced and Grace thought *great*. They were willing to pay the full price. Considering Grace was the listing agent there was no need for negotiating.

"I'll submit the paperwork to your attorney and we should be able to have you in by the end of April." She shook both of their hands and told them she was happy for them. "This is a great house."

Grace texted Hudson letting him know she would be on time. She drove to her townhouse, changed her clothes and jumped back in her car. First, she turned on the radio. Taylor Swift's "Look What You Made Me Do" was playing on the radio. Feeling giddy, she sang the words aloud. Then she opened the moonroof. It was still light out and the warm air felt good coming in from the top. After she made the right onto Hedley Farms Road, she looked out the passenger window and saw Hudson standing on the bottom step between the two boxwood planters. The grounds were spectacular, well-manicured and lush in shades of green and white. Hudson walked toward her as she parked her car in front of a long border of white narcissus. When he opened the door for her, she felt a flutter in her stomach.

"Every time I see you or even think about you, I get butterflies in the pit of my stomach."

He laughed. "That's a good sign, right?"

"Oh, yeah," she replied.

He extended his hand to her. "I have a surprise for you."

She smiled, tilting her head ever so slightly, got out, stood up and looked into his eyes. When he leaned in and kissed her on the lips, she blushed.

"Come on, dinner will be ready in an hour."

"I'll help you in a second. I want to tour the house first."

He looked at her and smiled. "Make all the changes you want," he said and headed for the kitchen.

"I don't want to change a thing, I am looking for some ideas for Ella and Ava," she called out to him and then walked into his study. The room was filled with rich cherry. The walls, ceiling and his desk boast the beautiful dark wood. Above his Apple computer she read his degrees. She noticed the fireplace still had ambers from the night before; above the couch was a photo of him standing next to his father and grandfather.

She felt him put one hand on her shoulder before handing her a glass of wine with the other. "They taught me the meaning of family."

She leaned her head back just enough to feel his body next to hers.

"They shared their love and the importance of in-home visits with me."

Grace turned to face him. "I wish I could have met them." She kissed him before taking her first sip. "I love that you see patients in here and in their homes."

He raised an eyebrow. "Imagine you are sick. The last thing you want to do is climb in your car and drive to go see your doctor."

She took him by the hand. Outside his office was the main house. Living room, dining room, family room, and kitchen all painted in shades of pale white with monochromatic decor. The kitchen nook was surrounded by windows overlooking the ocean. Beyond the back deck, a patio and the swimming pool. To the right a miniature golf course. Upstairs, there were five enormous ensuite bedrooms and an upper deck with ten lounge chairs and even more gorgeous views of the ocean. The master bedroom was over the downstairs nook because it too was surrounded by wraparound windows. At the end of the hall was a large library leading to the lower levels by a secret stairway. When they reached the bottom level, they entered the media room and finally the gym, complete with a wet bar and sauna.

Hudson touched the side of her face. "The moment you walked into The Stonebridge Restaurant; I knew I wanted to bring you home." He spun her around. "I just wish my mother was here to meet you. She would have loved you. Grace, you shall forever own my heart."

Her heart was racing. She had never felt this way before. No man had ever made her feel the way Hudson did.

She kissed him on the lips, took his hand and placed it over her heart. "Can you feel that?" She looked into his crystal blue eyes, waiting.

Hudson took hold of her and kissed her passionately, long and lingering until neither of them could breathe. "Grace, every time I see you, I am happier than the time before. Even my patients have noticed something different about me. One lady told me I had better marry the woman making my eyes sparkle." He laughed, "She's a writer. Everything she says is colorful."

Grace wanted to spend every day for the rest of her life with him in it. "I feel the same way about you."

He looked into her eyes. "Make all the changes you want."

She shook her head. "I don't want to change anything. I was thinking..."

The alarm was going off in the kitchen. They ran hand-in-hand up the stairs. Hudson turned off the alarm and asked her if she wanted another glass of wine or a cocktail. She asked what was on the menu before deciding.

"Ah, very good. Umm, Dungeness crab cakes with Meyer lemon aioli, Farralon salad—scallops, lobster tails, salmon and mixed baby greens with a champagne vinegar dressing. Followed by herb crusted seared prime rib."

She sat on a stool at the counter looking at him. "Are you for real?"

He laughed and said, "Bose, play country classics." Then he pointed to the wine cellar. "You decide."

She got up and said, "You slay me." She chose a bottle of Cabernet Sauvignon. When she returned, he had two glasses sitting on the counter. "Can I help?" She asked as she set the bottle down.

"Yes, check on the internal temperature of the roast while I open the wine?"

"Sure, how do you like your beef?" She opened the oven and took hold of the two oven mitts before setting the pan on the hotplate. She stuck the meat thermometer in and read, "One-forty-five."

"Perfect for me, how about you?" He replied as he set their glasses on the table in the dining room.

Grace walked up to him, placed her hands on his shoulders, kissed the back of his head and asked, "Can we eat in the nook?" Then she walked over to the table and picked up their dishes. "I want to sit as close to you as I can tonight."

First, Hudson made a toast to the two of them, then he lifted his fork and asked her to try the lobster tail. She graciously opened her mouth and accepted his offering. "Oh, my goodness!" She declared and stabbed a second bite for herself. Even better than the lobster were the scallops, but the salmon left her wanting more. "Everything is so delicious."

Hudson sat his fork down on the table, leaned back and smiled from ear to ear. "I have a confession to make."

Grace smiled at him. "You didn't cook. Did you?"

He put his napkin on his lap. "Yes, I cooked." He reached for her hand and kissed the back of it. "I have waited my whole life for you. To share my love of cooking with you, my passion for taking care of families. I want to share my life with you one story after another. To hear how your day was, talk about our future. I want to spend so many more days like this with you. Grace, I was so nervous about tonight, I—" He stopped himself remembering she wanted to do something with the house. He held his hand out to her. "Before the alarm went off you wanted to tour every room in the house, I want you to make whatever changes you want."

"No, changes." She put her hand on his arm. "I'm sorry, I wasn't looking to make any changes. I told Ella and Ava about the wood in your office and how wonderful it would look as a backdrop for their men's clothing line." She tilted her head. "Okay, I was looking to see if you had room for me. Would you allow me to set up my computer in the library. I was thinking I could work from here when I am not showing houses. I promise to be very quiet and I will even tippy toe by your office when you're with your patients." She blushed before adding, "Maybe, if they see me, they'll stop trying to find you a bride."

"That would make me very happy." Hudson beamed. "Whatever you want," he replied and caressed the back of her neck. "You can set up your laptop in my office if you want."

They both laughed.

A chill ran down her back. He made her feel good about what she was about to say, about everything in life. She smiled warmly at him, her chest rising and falling with every breath. Most of all she wanted children "Can I tell you something?"

"Anything," he replied.

"I have an appointment at a fertility clinic. More than anything in the world, I want a family. Hudson, do you want children?"

A Cheshire cat smile appeared on his face. "Is four too many?" Then he got down on one knee, reached in his pocket, opened the small box, took out the emerald-cut diamond en-gagement ring and asked her, "Will you marry me?"

Chapter Eleven

Grace caught her breath before it left her chest. Her eyes filled up fast. She dropped to the floor in front of him, hugged him and looked into his eyes. "Yes, I will marry you." Then she held out her hand while Hudson slipped the most gorgeous ring she had ever seen on her finger.

No one cleared the table or ate the crème brûlée. Hudson handed her the house phone. "Call them," he said and got up to open a bottle of champagne.

Grace was so nervous; she dropped the phone. She decided to use her cellphone and hit speed dial, linking Ava in on the call. When she told them she got engaged, Hudson laughed aloud hearing their joyful screams.

Grace could not stop crying. Ella and Ava, both told her they were happy for her and Hudson. "You make the perfect couple," Ella said and Ava agreed.

"Grace, we are so excited for the two of you. Oh my! When, where?" Ava asked.

"We haven't even talked about it yet. We wanted to call you first."

Hudson put his hands on her shoulders and whispered in her ear, "Do they know how much I love you?"

She kissed him on the cheek and said, "They know how much I love you." Then she glanced down at her ring and said, "Wait until you see my ring." As she held her hand out in front adding, "It is to die for."

Hudson handed her a glass of champagne and said, "To the most beautiful bride in the world."

Ella and Ava shouted, "Cheers."

"I'll see you tomorrow," Grace told them and ended the call.

Hudson and Grace took the bottle outside and sat on the back terrace, sipping, laughing and talking about having a small, elegant wedding. "Can we get married here?" She asked.

"Anywhere you would like," he replied. He kissed her and asked if she wanted to take her champagne down by the water. "I want to show you something."

Hand in hand they walked through the back yard until they reached the water's edge. On the other side of the inlet was a gazebo and a large pavilion. "How big is that?" She asked.

He smiled and pointed to the row boat. "Come on, I'll show you."

He helped her step in and handed her the bottle and his glass before grabbing the oars. The pavilion was sixty feet long by forty-five feet wide. There were four chandeliers, eight ceiling fans hanging down along with matching lanterns on every post. To the right was a huge fire pit with seating for thirty, beyond that a bar and a dance floor.

"My father held my mother's fiftieth birthday party here. If you would like…"

She kissed him long and hard. "I do."

"Are you sure, because there's always the rose garden."

She looked into his eyes and started crying.

"Aww, sweetheart, I hope those are happy tears?" he said and hugged her.

She buried her face in his chest. Five minutes had passed before she leaned back and told him he made her the happiest woman alive. "I was so scared. I thought I would never find someone to love me and want to have children with me. Hudson, you are a dream come true."

He took her face and held it in his hands. "I knew the first time I saw you that I wanted to spend the rest of my life with you. I have one request. Will you take a drive to New York City with me next weekend and meet my sister."

"I would love to meet your sister. Are the two of you close?"

He laughed before saying, "Yes, but we don't see each other as much as we should. She has three children and a very busy lifestyle."

"Tell me about her." She glanced away for a second. "Please." Then she took his hand and started to walk over to the line of Adirondack chairs.

They sat down, sipping wine while Hudson spoke about his family. "She's a doctor at New York Presbyterian Hospital."

"Does she live in the city?"

"Yes," he said and sat his glass down. "She owns a penthouse about fifteen minutes from the hospital on Riverside Drive. We are very different. She loves the fast pace, while I live for the everyday peace-of-mind knowing I will see my patients more often."

Grace nodded. "Yeah, working in a hospital you don't always get to see your patients again. Your patients are so blessed to have you."

"You are going to love Stefanie, she's the coolest doctor around. Her patients, staff and everyone who meets her immediately fall in love with her spunky personality. She wears these headbands featuring Disney characters from princesses to Minnie Mouse." Hudson held his phone out showing an article the New York Times ran on Dr. Stefanie Hong.

Grace held the phone up close. "She is adorable. Absolutely beautiful and yes, I love her headband."

That weekend, Grace and Hudson went to the ballet, and to Levitt Pavilion where they sat on the lawn and listened to Caleb Caudle—a rocking country-soul singer-songwriter sing bourbon-rich songs.

Grace rested her head on Hudson's shoulder listening to the soothing sounds of Caudle sing, "Red Bank Road."

His voice was so soothing she had tears in her eyes listening to him. Her heart could not have been happier, sitting there with the man she was about to be married to. Her dream of being a wife, mother and homemaker was about to come true.

"Hudson, would you mind if I stayed home until the children were all in school?"

He kissed the top of her head. "I was hoping you would say that. I didn't want to sound old fashioned, but I like the idea that you will be their first impression on the world." He leaned over and told her she didn't have to work. "If you want to work, I'm fine with it, but if you choose to stay home and host charity events for the community that would be great too."

"Did your mother stay home?" She asked.

"No, my mother was a doctor too. She worked at St. Vincent's Medical Center until she became the hospital administrator."

"I'm not smart enough to become a doctor," Grace replied.

Hudson spun her around. Shook his head and told her. "I never want to hear you doubt yourself again. You can do anything you put your mind to and Grace—I think you would make a great doctor."

She kissed him feeling embarrassed about allowing her self-doubt to be exposed. "Do you really think so?"

"Yes, I do," he replied and kissed her so passionately the man sitting to their right, jaw dropped. Hudson laughed, whispered in her ear. "We have an audience."

Grace sat up, brushed her blouse down and smiled. "It's our first date."

The man raised his eyes to the sky as if he didn't see anything.

Chapter Twelve

David was shocked when Ryan said he would go with him to tour the inn. "Thank you so much for going with me. Hell, for letting me do this."

Ryan cut the padlock with a pair of bolt cutters and just in case they needed a hacksaw he brought that too. "You have to swear to never tell anyone we are doing this," he said as he opened the gate.

David raised his right hand. "I swear." Then he followed Ryan inside. They were both shocked by what they saw. The entire lobby was in a shambles. "This makes me sick," David said as he bent down, picked up a chair and stood it back up. "Why would anyone allow this to happen?" The entire lobby was full of seagull droppings, papers were everywhere, furniture knocked down and dead plants crying out to be saved. "That railing has to go, but I'm glad the steel beams are still intact." When they reached the office David and Ryan could not believe their eyes. Files left open for everyone to read, credit card receipts lying on the floor, even thank you cards from previous guests. Credit card machines, room keys, mail even guest information tossed on the floor.

The pool area was the worst. The ivy had taken over the entire space. The pool was an empty cement hole, cracked and in poor condition. Sitting at the bottom—a lonely plastic white chair. The gym was stripped of all equipment. Graffiti on the walls. The guest's rooms seemed to be the only space still intact. Pictures bearing scenes of the ocean hung in every room. Beds stripped, dressers empty and bathrooms in need of a good cleaning. "We have to do something before that mold gets any worse," David said and Ryan agreed.

"Yeah, the board of health is going to have a field day with this place."

They were careful roaming the passageways from the inside leading to the rooms on the outside.

"Hey, I want to go back inside and see if we can find the boiler room."

"Okay," Ryan said. "Follow me, I think I know where it is." They went back downstairs, tried to open several doors in the hallway leading to the pool area.

Nothing.

Then David pulled on a door exposing the laundry room. "We have to be getting close."

"I can't believe it. The towels are still white," Ryan said until he touched one of them exposing yellow water stains. "EEK, that's nasty!" Then he pointed to the ceiling. "There's the problem."

David inhaled. "Yeah, I'll bet we discover a lot of leaks." Then he stepped into a dark corner.

"Hey, I think I found your boiler room," Ryan called out from across the hall.

When David banged on the fuel tank, he heard a hollow sound.

"Empty," Ryan said as he moved past the hot water tank and slop sink.

"Let's find the kitchen," David said as he closed the door behind them. They walked through the lobby and into one of the dining rooms before going into the kitchen.

"The stench is horrible in here. How the hell are you going to get the smell out?" Ryan shook his head. "I suppose you could use big fans and a million room deodorizers." Ryan pulled his shirt up over his nose.

David walked up to the coffee makers and said, "They're in good condition, I'm surprised no one stole them." Then he looked at the stainless-steel sinks, counters and work stations. "I'll have to rip the entire kitchen out and start new."

"Hey, I think this is the banquet room. Watch out, he's trying to get out." Ryan pointed to a sea gull flying above their heads.

David grabbed a chair, stood on it and told Ryan to direct the bird his way. Then with his bare hands he captured him and carried him out to the pool area so he could fly free.

After touring the entire property and discovering more neglect than an empty page in a novel, David knew he had to do whatever it took to rescue the inn.

"I wish I thought to bring a pad of paper and a pen. There is so much that needs to be done in here." Then David picked up a letter from a guest and read it aloud. 'Dear Management, we wanted to say thank you for your hospitality. We stayed on the top floor overlooking the swimming pool. Our room was clean, housekeeping was courteous and respectful. The amenities made our stay seem comfortable and even more enjoyable. After fishing all day, it was a pleasure to find a comfortable bed so close to the docks and to everything else Point Judith has to offer. We shall see you again next summer.' "Come on," David said. "The inn is screaming to be saved."

"I see what you're saying," Ryan said and then motioned for David to follow him outside. "What exactly are you hoping to do with the place, because from where I'm standing ... it doesn't look salvageable."

David thought long and hard before answering him. "Trust me, if I can't remodel, I will rebuild. I am not going to allow anyone to put in a parking lot. The fishing industry needs affordable housing."

Ryan put his hand on David's shoulder telling him, "If I can do anything else let me know. Just don't spend all your money."

Chapter Thirteen

Spring flowers were blooming in all of Hudson's gardens, and with every bloom, Grace became excited about their wedding plans.

Hudson reentered the kitchen feeling exuberant about his upcoming nuptials. "Grace, have you decided on a date yet?" He asked as he poured them both a second cup of coffee.

She walked up to him, kissed him on the cheek, held her cup out to him, smiled and replied, "I have always wanted to get married during the month of June." Then she took a sip of her coffee, hoping he felt the same.

Hudson set the coffee pot back on the warmer, turned to face her and responded by saying, "This June, right?"

"Yes, silly, on the eighteenth, if that is okay with you?" she blushed before adding, "The weather in June is perfect for an outdoor wedding."

He kissed her on the back of her head telling her he agreed wholeheartedly. "You are going to be a beautiful bride." Then he sat down next to her, took her hand in his and said, "And an even better wife and mother."

Her heart fluttered hearing the words. "I'd like to wait until after the wedding to try to conceive."

He smiled, told her he agreed one hundred percent and then took the last bite of his avocado toast.

She picked up their plates and whispered in his ear. "We can still have sex."

He shook his head. "Oh, no you don't. You're not taking advantage of me until after the wedding."

"Hudson, I am not waiting five weeks to have sex with you again." She motioned with her right hand pretending to be satisfying him orally when he jumped up and kissed her tenderly. Then he took her by the hand and led her outside onto the patio and into the swimming pool where they made love.

After a quick shower, they both went their separate ways. He had patients to see and she was meeting Ava and Ella to pick out dresses. "I love you more than you will ever know," he said to her as she walked out the front door and into her car. He loved having her there on the weekends. Lord knows he missed her terribly during the week. But he understood, she had clients to please and houses to sell. He waved goodbye one more time.

Grace blew him a kiss before driving down the driveway.

Grace was first to arrive at the bridal salon. The owner met her in the front room. Escorted her to a private room filled with gowns all in her size. "I would like to wait for my friends to arrive before I look," she told the woman.

"We're here," Ella said as she brushed her hand along one of the dresses.

While Ava and Ella were admiring all of the dresses, the store clerk told Grace she would be right back. She returned with a silver tray carrying three glasses of Mimosa and canapés.

"Thank you," Grace said as she accepted the first glass.

Ava helped herself to one of the appetizers before taking hold of her glass. "Cheers."

"To the most gorgeous bride in all of Connecticut," Ella added.

Grace kissed them both on their cheeks. "Thank you. Now help me find a dress."

"What is Hudson wearing?" Ava asked.

"We both liked your suggestion of the navy-blue suit with a satin edged notch lapel. So, I was thinking I would like to wear a short, ivory dress with a matching navy bow around my waist."

Ella held up two dresses. Ava shook her head and waved her hand toward her and said, "Too boxy."

Grace reached over and pulled down a satin dress with a halter top. They both said, "No way."

Ava looked through several dresses before holding up a gorgeous Vera Wang dress with a deep plunge neckline stopping at the waist. "Perfect!" She said and asked Grace to try it on.

In the meantime, Ella asked the owner if she had any satin ribbon in navy blue. When the woman came back holding three shades of navy and a pair of scissors, Ella thanked her. Before Grace stepped out of the dressing room, Ava had two more dresses for her to try on. One dress was more slip like and the other had too much lace, but Ella had another Vera Wang dress in her possession and that one had Grace's name written all over it.

Grace stood in front of the mirror as Ava tied the ribbon around her waist. They both shook their heads. "Nah," Grace said as she caught sight of the dress Ella was holding onto. "Ooo, let me try that one on."

Ava and Ella ate a few more appetizers, drank a second glass of Mimosa while waiting for Grace to pull back the curtain. "Grace?" Ella called out to her.

"Do you need help?" Ava asked.

They looked at each other. "Grace!" Ella shouted.

A second later, Grace appeared with tears in her eyes. "I love it," she said as she stepped in front of the mirror.

Ella wiped away her own tears and then moved closer to hug Grace as Ava tied one of the ribbons around her waist. The ribbon was perfect in size and color. The shop owner said they could take it with them to the next room while they looked at the men's suits.

"Are you okay?" Ella asked.

"I am so happy, I can't breathe. I am so blessed to have the two of you in my life and now I am getting married."

"Life is good," Ava said as she picked up her pocketbook.

Ella pointed to it and asked, "Is that an original?"

Ava's faced turned red as she held her pocketbook close to her chest. "Yes," she replied.

"Come on I want to look at suits and then take the two of you to lunch afterwards," Grace called out before stepping back in the dressing room. When she came back out, she handed the dress to the store owner and told her she was buying the dress. "I can pay for it now."

"What if you need any alterations," she replied accepting the dress with one hand and the ribbon in another.

"The dress fit perfectly and I have a pair of flats that will match just fine."

"Sounds good, let me put it in a garment bag for you and ring you up."

Grace turned to Ava and Ella and told them she wanted to buy their dresses as well. "I saw several dresses that I want the two of you to try on." She walked over to the next room and pointed to a rack of dresses similar to hers. Grace held up a dress that had a blue lace bodice and pointed to Ava. "What do you think?"

"I love it. Can Ella and I wear the same thing?"

"I was hoping," Grace replied and turned toward Ella. "Do you like it?"

"I'm sorry, I didn't catch the whole conversation. Like what? The dress? Sure," she replied with concern written all over her face.

"Do you want to wear the same dress as Ava?" Grace asked as she held up the dress.

"Whatever you want," Ella said and sat down on the bench.

Grace knew that look and so did Ava.

"Grace," Ava called out holding up a similar dress except that one had a lace skirt. "I can wear the lace top and Ella can wear this one."

"Maybe we should look at a few more," Grace said to Ava and nodded her head toward Ella.

"Ella, do you like this dress, or do you want to look at a few more?" Ava asked.

Ella stood up, clapped her hands together and said, "I love it. Seriously, I do."

"Can you both try them on so I can buy them today," Grace said in a low and concerning voice.

Ella looked at Ava's pocketbook one more time before accepting the dress from Ava and going into the dressing room.

They both came out at the same time and Grace once again had tears in her eyes as she cupped her hand over her mouth.

All three women hugged. Ella stopped in front of the mirror once more before going back in to take the dress off. "I'll buy our dresses," she called out and closed the curtain, but by the time she and Ava had stepped out of the dressing room, Grace had already paid for everything in cash.

"We can all go in my car or meet at the restaurant," Grace said when the clerk handed them each their garment bags. "Unless you have to get back to the boutique."

"Nope, we took the entire day off to spend it with you," Ella said.

"Yeah, this is your day," Ava announced.

"We'll follow you in my car," Ella said.

"Okay," Grace replied. "How about the Station House on Main?"

"Yes!" Ava said. "I love their sushi bar." She shrugged her shoulders. "Whatever you want."

Grace laughed. "I'm dying for sushi too. Ella you ready?"

Ella took a deep breath and blew it out slowly before holding her keys up. "Sure, let's go."

Ava and Ella helped Grace put her dress in her car then they got in Ella's car and followed her to the restaurant. "I think she chose the Station House Restaurant because it's close to our boutique and she knows you hate going too far when we're busy," Ava said as she turned the radio on.

Ella turned onto the main road following Grace's every lead. "Ava, can I ask you a question?"

Ava inhaled before saying, "Sure."

"Did Grace give you that pocketbook?"

"No, I was feeling down and I bought it to cheer myself up."

"That's fine, accept you took three advances on your salary during the first quarter because you were short on paying your rent. I'm just worried about your spending habits." Ella scratched her head. "You need to pay your bills first."

"Maybe, I should go to work with Grace and sell real estate."

Ella shook her head. "Grace receives all of her expensive merchandise from Geraldine Prescott. What are you going to do, steal her client?" Ella parked the car next to Grace's. "Just try to be a little more conscious about your spending. Okay?"

"Or find a rich man," Ava replied and got out of the car.

Ella took her by the arm. "I love you. I just don't want to see you get buried by debt."

The entire time they were listening to Grace talk about her big day, Ella pondered the idea of opening an account and paying all of Ava's bills.

"I want the two of you to find a man just like Hudson, he's perfect," Grace said as she set her napkin down on the table.

"We're so happy for you," Ella said and asked for the check. "Stop, I got this." She held up her hand as if to say don't argue with me.

"You better let her pay or she'll never forgive you," Ava said adding, "I saw a bakery on our way here. We can help you pick out your cake."

"I noticed it," Grace said. "You just want to go there because they had a cake with a Chanel pocketbook as a cake topper."

The ladies chose a four-tier vanilla cake with cannoli cream filling. "No topper," Grace said as she paid for the cake. "We both have a sweet tooth."

Grace bought a small round cake with a little brown teddy bear on it to take to Hudson's for the weekend. She asked if the woman could write, "I Can Bearly Wait!" on it.

"Okay, what else can we assist you with?" Ella asked as she followed Grace out of the bakery.

"Dance music," Grace said. "We need to come up with a playlist by Saturday"

"What kind of music does Hudson like?" Ava asked and sat down at one of the café tables outside the bakery.

Ella and Grace followed her lead and sat down. A minute later a waiter came out and asked if they wanted to see a menu. "Would you care for something to drink?"

Grace glanced at the menu and asked if they wanted to share the starter tray with mini Italian pastries on it and a cup of tea. "Do you want tea or something sweeter?" She asked.

"I'll have a chai latte," Ella said.

"Me, too," Ava said and set her pocketbook under the table.

"Just hot tea for me," Grace said. "Oh, can you bring me a piece of paper and a pen too?"

"Of course, I'll be right back."

They laughed over some of Grace's song choices. "We both like country."

"Since when?" Ella teased.

"Wait, I know! Here," Ava announced and handed her cellphone to Grace. "The one hundred most requested wedding reception songs."

Grace smiled when she read the first ten songs were country. "See."

Chapter Fourteen

The board meeting started out with an argument between one of the female town officials and an investor. "If I buy the land, I can do whatever I want with the property," she said and then added, "If...I want to put in a parking lot, I can and there's nothing you can do to stop me."

"No, Ma'am you can't," she said adding, "there are zoning regulations and restrictions on the property."

David let out a breath of relief as he observed the rest of the panel's expressions.

Sitting behind laptops at a long table were five board members, a secretary who seemed to be writing everything down, someone from the zoning department and another person from the legal department. They all looked puzzled, knowing they had a fighter on their hands.

An elderly man raised his cane and said someone should bulldoze the entire place down to the ground. "It's a disgrace. No one wants to walk by and see dead seagulls everywhere."

David noticed several of the board members look at one another. He wondered who was on board with rebuilding the inn and whom was against it.

"At this point I think we are all leaning toward tearing down the defunct inn," another board member said in response.

David stood up. "You can't be serious about bulldozing the inn. Excuse me, but isn't there anything we can do to stop the demolition? We need that inn."

The lawyer representing the town announced there was a proposed site plan in place, however there was not a deed restriction stating someone had to rebuild. "Actually, someone could tear down the inn and put in a parking lot."

"What inn?" Another board member asked. "The building is falling apart, there is mold everywhere and it would take a miracle to turn that place back to an inn. As it stands right now, we have one serious bid that we should consider." He smiled at the woman looking to tear down the inn. "Right now, no one wants to see another failed inn."

"What about the people who depend on the inn for their overnight guests?" David asked.

"You have got to be kidding me," the woman who wants to put in the parking lot said. "There are plenty of other places for people to stay in Point Judith."

David shook his head at her. "I'm sorry, I didn't catch your first name."

She smiled at him. "Geraldine," she replied and stood up as if she was ready to battle it out right there in front of everyone.

David gave her a wry grin. "Geraldine, please the boat captains depend on the inn for their anglers. The inn is a selling point for them. These men and women are tired after a long day out on the water. They deserve a place close by to get a good night's sleep."

"For goodness' sake, The Break Hotel is close by," Geraldine said and turned to leave.

Again, David shook his head, this time in disagreement. "They need affordable lodging. The Lighthouse Inn provided that for them. Your suggestion costs over four-hundred dollars a night."

She looked around the room. Glanced down at her notes and told him she was not backing down. "I have plans for that parcel and there's nothing you or anyone else can do to stop me."

"So do I," David said to her and then turned his attention to the board members. "All I am asking is you give me a shot. Tell me what you want. Give me the requirements and let me save the inn. Come on people. The Lighthouse Inn is a staple in Point Judith. I grew up in that place. We all did." He pointed to the lawyer at the end of the table. "You never missed a Friday swim class. I remember seeing you there every Sunday for brunch."

The lawyer moved his pen. "There's a lot that needs to be considered."

"Good!" David said a little louder than intended. "Now tell me what needs to be done."

"Well, to start you'll have to meet with the hazmat team to develop a plan to remove all of the asbestos before any construction can be done. No one is to go inside until every last ounce of contamination is removed." He shook his head. "It's not cheap. And no matter who buys the place." He shrugged his shoulders. "It will have to be done before a bulldozer or man steps foot in the place."

"What else?" David asked.

"Well, you could sign the petition Dr. Al Alba started," the secretary said. "He too is looking for a revitalization plan."

"Thank you," David said to her and wrote her name down.

Someone new walked in wearing what appeared to be a very expensive business suit. Stood next to Geraldine and asked, "When will the bidding begin?"

"We have to wait until the lessee's lease is up. As of right now he's only in contempt for the lack of care for the property."

Geraldine glanced over at David before telling the man, "I'm not backing down. I'm putting in a parking lot." Then she pointed to David and said, "He wants to save the damn place."

David motioned to the lawyer. "So, someone could actually tear down the inn and put in a parking lot and there is nothing any of you can do?" He said sounding even more irritated by what he just heard Geraldine tell her friend. With determination in his voice, he looked directly at Geraldine and said, "I will fight you in court if I have to."

The secretary motioned for David to go out the side door. A minute later she told him to follow her to the office. He asked where he could sign the petition. "Thanks for telling me about the petition, I'd like to sign it. I can't thank you enough for telling me about it."

"I have it in my desk, but don't tell anyone. Dr. Alba said we don't need any more parking lots and I agree with him. I also liked how you said rebuilding will help save the fishing industry. We need to help as many local businesses as we can and while we're at it, our tourism. No one wants to see a parking lot when they come to Galilee." Then she handed him a proposed site plan. "This was approved six months ago, then Prescott came along with her idea of a parking lot and everyone pushed it under the rug."

David signed the petition and thanked her for her assistance. He tucked the plan in his folder and waved goodbye. The next day, he sent her a fruit basket from The Fruit Company in Oregon so no one would know it was from him.

Chapter Fifteen

Grace was so excited about moving in with Hudson, she donated all of her furniture to goodwill. The day she put her townhouse on the market it sold in a bidding war. The only thing she was taking to Hudson's home was, her laptop and wardrobe. Hudson had arranged for a moving company to pack her belongings and deliver them to his house the following Saturday. He didn't want to wait until the closing to be with her.

Friday evening, she stood in the doorway, looking back at her first purchase. She could have bought a small house with her money, but in the beginning, she wanted something cozy and near her office. Now, she schedules all her appointments on her laptop and, on occasion from her car. It will be nice to be able to work from home, book new listings with her feet up while relaxing by the pool, or in one of the many gardens and to be near the love of her life. She hugged herself. *Husband.* Grace has never felt this good about a word in her entire life. "I am getting married!" She said aloud and laughed as she closed the door behind her.

That evening Grace and Hudson celebrated with a cookout near the pool. Ava, Ella and Melvin all agreed they needed dance music since it was a dance floor that brought them all together. Ava didn't mind being the fifth person. She was happy she could be there for Grace. She was excited to see Ella had found someone too. She wasn't about to tell them her secret, not yet, anyway. She had to be sure Phillip was the one. Ella and Grace both seemed happy, perhaps it was time she too settled down. She liked him very much and he seemed to be happier each time they were together. Her only concern was his wardrobe. Phillip loved pastels. Not that men don't look good in pink; he just didn't know how to match his trousers with his shirts. They always clashed.

Grace clapped her hands. "Hudson, let's take everyone over to the ceremony site."

The weather was perfect for an evening stroll. Hand-in-hand Hudson and Grace led the way to the boat dock. Hudson walked past the row boat and opened the two big doors at the boathouse exposing a twenty-foot party barge. Once inside, he told everyone to climb aboard. Once again, Grace was in awe.

"What?" He said. "The row boat is too small for this many people."

She kissed his lips and noticed the bar. "You even stocked it with my favorite wine?"

"For you, I will stock it with baby wipes." He held out his hand for her to climb aboard.

Grace smiled at Ella and told her she was going to love it, then she put her arm around Ava and said, "You can decorate the pavilion anyway you see fit. Wait until you see the dance floor." She started to tell them about the chandeliers, but when Hudson came within sight of the island, everyone's mouths dropped open. It was even more beautiful than the first time Grace had seen it. It was during the golden hour and the glow was radiant.

Everyone got off the party boat and headed straight for the pavilion.

Like a schoolgirl showing her new saddle shoes, Grace practically ran over to the archway. Hugging one of the poles she declared her heart knew she had to get married up there. When she turned around to reach for Hudson, she noticed he was sitting down near the fire pit. She felt a gentle nudge in her stomach and went over to sit by him. He reached for her hand and asked if she was happy. She sat on his lap and told him, "I am the luckiest woman in the world. Of course, I am happy. I love you so much. I am going to make you happy every day for the rest of your life, Dr. Harbor."

"You have no idea how blessed I feel right now." He kissed her twice telling her to go have fun. "They're waiting for you."

"I love you."

She got up and hugged Ava and Ella before telling them how grateful she was to have them stand up for her.

"How many guests?" Ava asked.

"Between Hudson's family and friends and my own, we should have approximately one-hundred and fifty guests."

"The place is perfect," Ella said.

Ava, Ella and Grace decided on the color of the flowers, the greenery and the aisle runner. "I definitely, want white rose petals," grace announced and then announced she wanted a touch of navy blue.

"More ribbon," Ava asked.

"I was thinking for the flowers," Grace replied.

"Oh? Good, because we both love our dresses," Ava said adding, "blue delphinium comes in shades of light and dark blue."

"Perfect," Grace said.

"How about hydrangea, sea holly, and mascara?" Ella said raising her eyebrows.

Grace smiled remembering Ella always played florist when they were younger.

When they returned back to the boat Melvin explained he had several meetings to prepare for. Ella was meeting with a new supplier and Ava had a large delivery coming in the morning. "We're offering a new line of scarves," she said and gave Grace a kiss on the cheek. "We'll see you next weekend to go over the final details for the wedding."

"Okay," Grace replied adding, "Hudson and I are meeting with the caterer once more for a taste testing tomorrow, after that we are all set."

On the way back to the house Hudson told Grace he was going to call his heart doctor in the morning. "I usually go in September, but the other day when we were hiking in Sherwood Island, I noticed I had a hard time breathing on the slightest hills."

"Maybe, your allergies were flaring up. That happens to me sometimes." *Is that why he sat down earlier?* "Would you mind if I go with you?"

"I would like that," he said and poured them each a glass of chardonnay.

Several times Grace glanced over at Hudson. Each time she thought he appeared fine, but still she was worried. "Are you feeling overwhelmed by all the wedding plans?"

"No, that's the bride's job," he said and refilled her glass. "I would have been happy eloping."

Grace tossed her napkin at him. "Stop it! You were the first person to write down names on the guest list."

He laughed. "I had to shut those ladies up." Then he raised his hand in the air. "I'm kidding." He held his hand out for her to sit next to him. "Come here I want to tell you something."

Grace smiled ever so lightly before getting up and sitting on his lap. When Hudson kissed the nap of her neck, she thought her insides were going to explode. He whispered in her ear, "I love you more than you will ever know. I have waited my whole life for you."

"And I have been dreaming about you since I was a little girl."

Chapter Sixteen

Grace sat in the kitchen drinking her coffee. Hudson was taking longer than usual in the shower. He was confident the procedure would go smoothly. He told her it was a simple angiogram. Hudson explained it as a very common type of X-ray used to examine blood vessels that don't show up clearly on ordinary X-rays.

"Good morning, my love," Hudson said as he entered the kitchen.

Grace leaned her head back for a kiss. "Hudson, will you explain the procedure to me one more time."

"They inject a special dye into the area being examined. Sometimes they go through the vein in your wrist, but today they will be going through my groin. The dye highlights the blood vessels as it moves through them. It's such a simple procedure I'll receive a general anesthetic to numb the area so it doesn't hurt when they make a small cut in my skin to insert the catheter. I should be out of surgery anywhere from one to two hours."

"Are there any risks?"

"The benefits always outweigh the risks. If I have a blockage, they will see it immediately."

She sat up straighter. "What if they find blockage?"

"They'll remove it. Hopefully, they can treat it with medicine." He kissed her on the cheek. "Don't worry, I'll be fine." He winked at her. "Just don't make me chase you down the aisle."

She swatted the air. "I feel bad I chose Sherwood Island. If you didn't feel good that day, you should have told me. We didn't have to go hiking."

"Grace, sweetheart, I'll be fine. It's probably due to my lifestyle. I promise, I'll start using the gym right after the wedding."

She set her cup on the counter and rinsed the coffee pot. Hudson wasn't allowed to eat or drink anything prior to his procedure so she skipped breakfast and opted for a quick cup of coffee.

Hudson drove to the hospital, parked in the upstairs garage and took hold of Grace's hand as they entered the admitting room. After completing his paperwork, they were sent to a waiting room before going to a private room where Hudson was told to put on a hospital gown. The anesthesiologist came in first followed by two surgeons. They explained the procedure to Grace, ensuring her of their success rate. "Relax, he's in good hands," Dr. Peck said to her before telling Hudson he would see him soon.

A moment later, a nurse came in and asked Grace to wait outside the room. She needed to prep Hudson, give him a sedative and pack up his belongings. When she opened the curtain, she told Grace she could wait in the downstairs waiting room, where she could watch the board and follow the procedure. "You'll be able to see when they start and when they have completed the angiogram."

Grace pursed her bottom lip and gave Hudson a warm smile and a thumbs up. He reached out his hand and kissed the back of it before telling her, "I'll see you in a little while."

Grace kissed his lips. Looking into his eyes she told him, "I love you so much."

A male nurse walked in singing, "Piano Man" smiled and said, "It's show time!"

Grace moved out of his way as he took hold of the foot of the bed. The female nurse reminded Grace to go to the first floor waiting room. Grace thanked her, but as soon as they rolled the bed down the hall her stomach plummeted. She never did like hospital environments. When she arrived, there was no one in the waiting room. She stared at the screen. She could see the different surgical rooms, doctor's names and patients first initial and last name. When she read, "H. Harbor" she sat down. Several times she glanced up at the screen. A minute later a man came in and sat down across the room. He never took his eyes off the screen. Grace opened her phone and read the caterers reply. Everything Grace and Hudson picked out for the wedding was available and in season. They knew they were ordering too much, but they didn't care. They wanted it to be perfect. For their guests to be satisfied and they both knew what they liked. From the fish appetizers to the vegetable pakoras to the sorbets and chia pudding cups. She read the list again to make sure everything they wanted was on there. Lobster salad with butter lettuce cups, blinis with caviar and smoked salmon, roasted pear and mixed green salad, roasted chicken, steak and tuna tartar. The caterer even provided the perfect tablescape. She looked up at the screen again to see if he was out of surgery. Then she answered Ella's email telling her Hudson was still in surgery.

A moment later, Melvin walked in the door. "Ella said he went in an hour ago."

Grace patted the seat next to her. "Yes, he said it could take anywhere between an hour to two hours."

The man sitting across from them got up and walked out. Grace assumed his wife was S. Sawyer because his eyes were glued to that name.

"Aren't you supposed to be at work?" She asked.

Melvin explained that he has known Hudson since pre-school. "We have been through a lot together," he said. "The death of our parents to Hudson's grandmother who adopted me when my parents were robbed and shot in cold blood outside the Danbury Fair Mall."

Grace looked at him. "I'm so sorry," she said and hugged him. "Hudson admires you so much. You were the first person he insisted on attending our wedding."

"He loves you more than anything in the world. I have never seen or heard him talk about a woman as much as he does you. You brought the smile back to his face. You know half of his guests are the women who have been trying to fix him up with their daughters, granddaughters, and every single woman in Connecticut."

Grace laughed. "He told me. I hope they like me."

Melvin gave her shoulder a squeeze. "Trust me, they are going to love you."

Grace looked up at the board. H. Harbor was still there along with eight different names. Then she looked at her watch. Three and a half hours had passed. When her cellphone rang, she jumped. Without looking she said, "Hello."

"How is he?" Ella asked.

"He's still in surgery," she replied.

"We're on our way," Ella said and the call ended before Grace could tell her Melvin was with her and she was fine.

"Ella and Ava are coming down. I'm sure he's okay," she said sounding as if she was trying to convince herself.

Melvin stood up and said he was going to go to the front desk and get a report as to why it was taking so long. "A friend of mine had the procedure done a year ago and he was in and out under two hours." He stopped in the doorway and asked if she wanted anything to eat or drink.

She shook her head. "Thanks, I'm okay for now." Once again, her stomach plummeted.

Fifteen minutes later, Melvin returned with Ava and Ella. They both hugged Grace so tight she could hardly move.

"Sit down," Ella said and pointed to the seat on Grace's right for Ava. "He'll be fine. The nurse told Melvin they may have found some blockage and they are repairing it right now."

Melvin sat next to Ella and explained, "I asked the nurse to go upstairs and see what is taking so long."

Grace leaned forward. "Thank you." When Grace looked at the board his name had been removed. "He's out of surgery," she declared. "His name is not listed anymore." She took a deep breath and let it our slowly. "Thank God."

A half hour later, three doctors and a hospital administrator came in and asked for Grace. Grace held her hand up. "I'm Grace."

One doctor took hold of her hand and said, "I'm sorry, I did everything I could. Dr. Harbor suffered a massive heart attack. We tried everything to save him."

Another doctor tried explaining how it could have happened, but she collapsed to the floor before anyone could catch her. Melvin picked her up and held her in his arms. Tears were streaming down his face. Ella and Ava hugged each other as they too became weak in the knees. When the doctors offered to show them to a private room, Melvin demanded Grace be allowed to see Hudson. "Immediately," he said.

The men walked out of the room and said they would send in a nurse to escort her. When the nurse entered the room, she closed the door behind her, telling Grace she needed to get a copy of the video. "They videotape all procedures, especially when they are training a new physician."

Melvin read her name tag, Angel. Thanked her for her honesty. Ella reached over and hugged her. Ava passed out. The nurse opened the door and called for someone to bring in a bag of ice and smelling salts. A male nurse held the ammonia inhalant up to Ava's nose and she immediately woke up. Sobbing she asked if it was true. "Was he murdered?"

The nurse just looked at her. "Are you feeling better," he asked.

"I've got this," Ella told him and then put her arm around Ava. "Let's go." Then she whispered in her ear, "Shush."

Melvin wrapped his arm around Grace's body and held her close as they followed Angel down the hall. She pushed the button on the elevator and told them to get off on the tenth floor, they're waiting for you. Someone will take you to him. I told them to let you go in with her. She pointed to Melvin. Then she told Ella to be persistent.

Ella nodded and told her, "Thank you. I'll tell them we're his sisters."

Angel winked as she waved goodbye. When she made eye contact with Grace, she told her, "Be strong."

Grace reached out her arms and they hugged while Melvin held the door open. When they reached the tenth floor, two nurses were waiting by the elevator to take them to the operating room. Ella told Melvin to take care of her, while she stayed with Ava.

As soon as they were out of sight, Ella told Ava not to say a word about what the nurse had told them.

An hour later, Melvin came out carrying Grace in his arms. When he winked at Ella, she knew he had gotten a copy of the tape.

Grace had no words. Someone put a wheelchair in front of Melvin to make Grace sit down. Another person asked if she could have a word with Mrs. Harbor. Ella told her now is not the time. The social worker handed Ella her business card. "If she needs anything at all."

"We're fine," Ella told her and turned to leave.

They agreed to ride in one car. Ella drove while Ava sat in the back seat with Grace in her arms. Several times, Ella glanced in the rear-view mirror making sure Ava did not talk about anything. Before she reached Hudson's house, she noticed Melvin was sobbing. Grace must have heard him too because she reached up and patted his shoulder. With one hand he reached back and squeezed Grace's fingertips.

Ella heard her tell Ava, "Melvin and Hudson have known each other since pre-school."

Ava sat in her own silence before saying, "I'll stay with you tonight. We both will," she added and Ella agreed.

"We'll figure this out together," Ella said and then reached over and held Melvin's hand the rest of the way. When she pulled into the driveway, Grace lost all control, and so did Melvin. Ella thought about taking them to her house, but she needed to take a break herself. They sat in the driveway for what seemed like forever. Then Ella decided it was time to go inside. "It's getting dark, let's go inside, I'll make a pot of coffee."

Chapter Seventeen

Hudson's sister Stefanie told Grace she could stay in the house as long as she needed to. His sister had no desire to live in Connecticut. Grace thanked her for the opportunity, but explained it would be too hard to stay there without him. Grace stayed with Ella for the first two weeks after the funeral. She gave notice at the office, letting them know she was taking the summer off. She rented a house in Point Judith from June to the end of August.

"Are you sure?" Ella asked her. "You can stay here for as long as you need to."

"Salty Brine Beach will be good therapy for me. Please don't take this wrong, but I need to be alone."

Ella hugged her and told her she totally understood. She didn't mean to cry, but just thinking about Grace without Hudson, alone in Rhode Island her heart hurt. Grace kissed Ella on the forehead and told her they could visit her. "Bring Ava for a long weekend. We'll do yoga on the back deck, swim in the ocean and take long walks on the beach."

Ella smiled, wiped her nose with the back of her hand and replied, "I hope we are going to eat a ton of seafood."

They both laughed. Grace's laughter turned to tears. "My heart hurts. I wanted to spend forever with him. I love him more than you know." Her cellphone rang causing them both to jump. "It's Melvin. Hello."

Ella sat down in the living room. Grace followed her and sat next to her on the couch. "Yes, she's here too." Grace's hand went to her mouth.

Ella sat up; eyes wide as she stared at Grace.

"Hang on Melvin, let me put you on speaker."

Ella put her arm around Grace as they listened to Melvin explain he hired a lawyer. "The videotape shows the lead surgeon allowed the intern to perform the procedure. It appears he punctured Hudson's blood vessel. I'm not a doctor, but listening to the nurse in the background, she clearly says to both doctors, 'you ruptured the blood vessel, he's hemorrhaging.' Then someone else said something about the blood clot causing the heart attack."

Grace dropped the phone. Ella picked it up and told Melvin to keep her posted. Grace heard her tell Melvin, "Hey, Grace is going out of town for a few months, call me with your findings and I'll fill her in as needed."

Grace slid to the floor. Ella followed her lead and hugged Grace ever so tight. An hour later, Ella got up and made a pot of tea for them. While she was waiting for the water to get hot, she texted Ava to update her and let her know she would not be going to the boutique that morning. When she returned to the living room, Grace was sitting up hugging her knees to her chest. Ella set the tray on the coffee table and sat across from Grace.

Grace gave her a weary smile. "I was only with him for four months and that is all it took for me to know I wanted to spend the rest of my life with him. Every day was special. He made me feel like I was the only woman in the room. I meant something to him. He told me he loved me on our third date."

Ella reached for a tissue. "I'm so sorry. I hate seeing you like this. Tell me what I can do to make you feel better."

Grace reached for one of the tea cups, smiled warmly and said, "There is nothing anyone can do now. He's gone. I'll have to learn to live without him."

Ella nodded. Sipped her tea and said, "He loved you so much. You made his final days complete." She set her cup back down, inhaled deeply and added, "Grace?" Grace's face was pale. Ella feared she said the wrong thing. "I said that with love in my heart."

"I hope you are right. I will always be grateful for that dance and for every second I got to spend with him."

The next day, Grace followed Ella to the boutique to say goodbye to Ava. She promised them both she would be okay. "I just need a little time," she said as she waved to them and drove away. She knew better than to look in her rearview mirror. The only other time the three women have been separated was when Grace went away for two weeks to get her real estate license.

She was on I95 when the booking agent texted her saying the house would not be ready until six that evening. She glanced at the clock and noticed it was a quarter to eleven. She didn't care. Nothing bothered her. She was lost in her own thoughts. In eighteen days, she was supposed to be married to the love of her life. She knew right then and there on the dance floor that she wanted to spend forever with Hudson. She could not let go of him. The way he looked into her eyes, his gentle touch, smile and when he told her he loved her, her heart came to life with dreams of being with him, being a mother and yes living happily ever after.

She arrived in Point Judith at twelve-thirty. More than finding something to eat, she needed to stretch her legs and go to the bathroom. She parked her car next to the outdoor shower and restrooms. As soon as she sat on the toilet something sent a chill down her spine. When she glanced up, she saw a man looking down at her from the other stall. Grace yelled, quickly wiped herself, pulled her underwear up and ran out the door in time to stop a little girl from going inside. She picked the child up and told her not to go in there before setting her down on the ground. The girl's father asked Grace what was going on. When she explained there was a man inside, the man told the little girl to go and get her mother. "Run, sweetheart."

The little girl came back with a female Rhode Island State Police Officer. the little girl's father pointed to Grace and said, "She said there's man peeking over the top of the stalls."

A moment later, the police officer came out with a man in handcuffs. She stopped to thank Grace. "Thank you so much for protecting our little girl." She winked. "I got this."

The little girl touched Grace's hand before giving her a hug. Grace held back her tears. She was shaken by what could have happened. The girl's father shook Grace's hand thanking her. Then he went inside with his daughter.

Grace walked away as people gathered to see what all the fuss was about. She Googled best clam chowder in Point Judith and Aunt Carrie's Restaurant came up. It was about three miles down the beach. "Perfect." She tossed her wallet in her backpack along with her baseball cap and sunscreen. Walking by George's of Galilee the smell of food almost made her stop, but when she caught sight of a couple going in and holding hands, she kept walking toward the beach. Once she reached the beach she tossed her flip flops in her bag with the rest, put on her sunglasses and headed down the beach. Looking out at the ocean made her long for Hudson even more. She wished he was there strolling alongside her, holding hands and teasing her about baby names. They had wanted a honeymoon baby. She smiled thinking about Hudson hoping for two sets of twins. He said he would have been happy to be a girl dad as long as they all looked like their mother. Hudson was perfect in every way.

Whenever she saw happy couples, she focused on the waves, sailboats and the bright sun beaming on her face. Several times, she looked up hoping he was with her. Knowing how much she loved him. She missed him and wished they had one more moment together.

When she reached Aunt Carrie's Restaurant the first place, she needed to visit was the bathroom. She stepped up to the counter and ordered a bowl of chowder, the fried strip clams and a water with lemon. As tempting as the lobster roll looked, she thought about getting it another day. She took her food outside and sat in one of the Adirondack chairs looking out at the ocean. Before taking her first bite she took a picture of her view and bowl of chowder to send to Ava and Ella. "I made it. It is breathtaking. I'll call you as soon as I get settled into the house."

She didn't receive a reply and assumed they were busy with customers. There store was always swamped during the summer months, especially on the weekends.

After she ate, she took her cup and headed back down the beach. She knew the house was within walking distance from George's. She was halfway there when she became parched. Her cup was empty. It had to be at least ninety degrees outside and walking directly in the sun made it even hotter. She was so thirsty, she thought about squeezing the lemon in her mouth. Her cellphone was ringing and buzzing in her backpack. She knelt down, opened it up and answered Ella's call. "Hey," she said and sat down.

"We got your message. How's it going?"

"Great, Point Judith is breathtakingly beautiful."

"Are you settled in? Is the house as nice as the photos?" Ella asked.

"I don't know yet. The listing agent sent me a text and said the house won't be ready until this evening."

"What?" Ella yelled in the phone. "Why?"

"I don't know. Maybe the last person checked out late or left a mess. I'm fine. I may change into my bathing suit and go for a swim. The water is warm. But first I have to get something to drink. I'm dying of a thirst."

"Probably from the clams," Ella replied. "Okay, call me tonight."

"We miss you." She heard Ava yell in the background.

"I miss you too," she replied and put her cellphone in her pocket.

Grace walked down the beach listening to waves crashing on shore, watching seagulls dive for crumbs and feeling the warmth of hot sand under her feet. Finally, she moved close enough to the water to cool her legs off. When she saw the jetty, she knew her car was not that far up ahead. Then she looked at her cellphone and noticed she still had a few hours before she could go to the house, sadness fell all around her. "Why?" She cried out.

Chapter Eighteen

G race sat down on the beach and rested for an hour. She looked at her cellphone again to check the time and read a message from Steven. "Thank you for everything. The kids love the new house. I brought them to the closing hoping to introduce them to you, but one of your colleagues said you were away on vacation. Enjoy yourself and thank you again. If there is anything I can do for you please call."

Then she read her other messages, cleared most of them and answered a few before setting her automatic reply to read: "Out of the office until further notice."

Scrolling through her voicemails she came across the first message Hudson left for her. She listened to it several times, crying harder each time. She shut her phone off, put it back in her backpack and hugged her legs to her chest. "I love you so much," she cried. Tasting her salty tears, remembering the last time she tasted them was when he put the engagement ring on her finger. She cried happy tears telling him how much she loved him and how happy he made her. A warm breeze pushed her hair in front of her face. When the salty air moved the hair back something told her to get up and pull herself together. Hudson would not want to see her like this. He dedicated his life to making people feel better. He would want her to live her best life.

Up ahead, she noticed a man standing on an upper deck looking out at the ocean. Several times, he glanced her way and smiled. Grace nodded once. When she was close enough to hear him, she heard him say, "I would be more than happy to fill that cup for you. I have San Pellegrino and a very nice white wine in the fridge."

She was dying for something to drink. As if someone was pushing her from behind, she took two steps to the right, toward him. Grace looked up at him one more time before saying, "The sparkling water sounds great. Thank you."

He motioned for her to come upstairs. When she reached the top step, he held the gate open for her and said, "Take a seat, I'll grab a bottle and two glasses." When he returned, he set the bottle down and handed her a glass. On the tray was a dish with lemon slices and a bowl of ice. "I'm David."

She held her hand out to him and said, "Grace." Then she emptied her glass and laughingly said, "I cannot tell you how thirsty I was. Thank you so much."

David also laughed, telling her the sun will do that to you. "It's pretty hot today." He noticed she had a little sun burn on her cheeks. "How long have you been walking in the sun?"

Grace shook her head and replied, "Too long."

David lifted the bottle, Grace nodded and held up her glass. "Are you hungry?" He asked as he filled her glass.

"No, thank you. I had lunch at Aunt Carrie's. Would you mind if I used your bathroom?"

David stood up and pointed to the kitchen. "Straight through the kitchen, down the hall and it's the first door on the right."

Grace sat down on the toilet and gasped before pulling out her cellphone. *Identical!* She put her hand to her mouth, she thought the kitchen looked familiar too. "No," she told herself. But then when she reached the hallway and saw the photo of a boy swimming in an indoor pool, she knew. Before going back outside she took notice of the slate blue kitchen cabinets and brass knobs that looked like fishing hooks. She stepped out on the deck, hands on her hips and asked, "Is this a joke?"

David pulled his chin in, stood up and replied, "Excuse me?"

Grace held her cellphone out to him. "What are you doing here?" She demanded.

"I'm sorry. I'm not sure I know what you're talking about."

"The house! You rented the house to me, told me to come later and for what so you could get me drunk on wine and...get out!" She yelled. "You need to leave or I am calling the cops."

David had no idea what was going on. She appeared to be mad about something. He wondered if maybe she was on some sort of drugs.

Grace looked over at the fireplace and saw the photos, and noticed the two bronze horse sculptures were the same as the ones on her phone. She showed them to David and he almost fell over backwards.

"How did you get that picture? Who are you?" He demanded and then asked if he could take a closer look.

She handed him her phone and said, "When I rented the house from you, I told you I needed to be alone."

"You rented my house? From me?" He said and handed her back her phone. "Grace, please tell me what is going on."

She looked at him. His voice *was* different from the last time she spoke to the listing agent. "I rented the house for the summer."

"Grace, I never would have rented my house to you or anyone else. There has to be a misunderstanding. I'm sorry."

"You're sorry?" She yelled. Before adding, "I paid twenty-seven-thousand dollars for the place and all you can say is you're sorry. What about my money?" Her voice cracked with emotion.

"Believe me, I don't have your money. Can we please sit down and try to figure this out together?"

Grace wasn't amused. She asked if she could go outside and look at the front door. She knew the house number was on the right next to a black metal light fixture. "I need to look at your front door."

David followed her, in fact he almost walked into her when she stopped and showed him the photo of his door, he could not believe what was happening.

"Grace, someone has taken advantage of you and I promise you, I will get to the bottom of it. Please come inside and let's figure this out together."

Grace bent down, lifted the Welcome mat and took hold of the key. When she held it up David told her to see if it fit. "I have no idea how that got there," he said as he watched her open and close his front door.

After what happened earlier in the day, nothing surprised her. "I should just go," she said sounding disappointed.

David went to put his hand on her shoulder, but instead opened the door wider. "Please, I want to help."

Grace heard compassion in his voice. "Okay, maybe it wasn't you," she said and stepped inside.

"Believe me. It was not me. Now please start from the beginning." Then he pointed to the living room sofa.

Grace who had been an emotional mess all day, sat down in the accent chair and told him she rented the house from Dunkin Cottage Realty. She talked to the listing agent and explained she wanted to rent the house for the summer. "He told me he had the perfect summer house from June to the end of August."

David had a perplexed look on his face when he said, "You mean Durkin, right?"

Grace looked at the ad and replied, "No. It says Dunkin." Then she showed him all of the text messages.

David pulled out his cell and showed her the same picture, except his photo was the actual agency in town. "Grace, you have been scammed. How did this person find you?"

Grace's face was burning red. David was not sure if it was her day in the sun or if she was about to blow. "I'm a real estate agent. How did I not see this?"

"Grace, can I have his cellphone number please?"

"Why?"

"Let me have the cellphone, email and anything else you have. I know a private detective."

"Do you have a printer?" Grace asked and stood up.

"Yes," David replied and got up. "Upstairs in my study, I have two printers."

Grace followed him. "Great it's an HP," she said and printed all of her conversations.

David took hold of the papers, looked them over and dialed a phone number. Grace listened as David explained a friend of his was scammed by someone and he needed to find the person. "The fool rented my beach house to her for a lot of money. Call me as soon as you find him. Yes, I know he could be in Pakistan. Thanks."

When David hung the phone up, he saw Grace had moved to one of the port windows. "The view is spectacular from up here," she said before turning back around.

"Thanks, I have always had a passion for lighthouses. I wanted this room to resemble a beacon of hope. I had it built a few years after I inherited the house from my parents. I leave the light on hoping they know I am still taking care of the place."

Grace looked into his eyes and saw the love he had for his parents. "That is so sweet of you."

David's stomach growled. "Excuse me," he said, adding, "I was planning on having lobster rolls for dinner, you're welcome to join me."

After walking on the beach all afternoon, she was hungry. He seemed nice enough and she wanted to hear what his friend had to say about the person who took her money. "Wait, first let me look at my PayPal account." She logged on and saw the money had all been transferred into his account. Even the photo on his PayPal was the same as his email's. She shook her head. "How did I not notice the spelling?" She threw her hands up in the air. When her stomach echoed his she said, "I would love a lobster roll. Thank you."

David grinned. "Great!" He motioned for her to go back downstairs as he explained he had plenty of room for her and he was even willing to leave. "You can stay here as long as you need to."

She stopped short and he almost walked into her a second time. She turned to face him. "I would never put you out of your home. I'll go to a hotel."

David smiled and explained it would not be easy that time of the year. "We'll talk about it over dinner."

She made eye contact with him. "As soon as I get my money back, I am going to..." she took a deep breath. "Beat the crap out of that guy."

Chapter Nineteen

Grace took her first bite. The last time she had a lobster roll was when her, Ella and Ava went to Cape Elizabeth in Maine. While Ava and Ella, both got theirs with mayonnaise, Grace opted for the buttered version. She closed her eyes remembering how much she loved the sweet savory taste. "Mmm," she said and opened her eyes. "Oh, my goodness this is fabulous."

"I'm glad you like it," he said and offered to pour her another glass of lemonade.

"Please," she said and held her glass up.

"I hope you don't mind my aunt is stopping by in a little while. Every Thursday she drops off a sampling of her desserts." He laughed. "If I am lucky, she'll have a few other dishes as well."

"I can go out on the deck; besides I should probably start looking for a hotel room."

David shook his head. "Grace, I have plenty of room for you right here. Five bedrooms, three bathrooms and I spend most of my day in my study."

"Are you sure?" It was seven-thirty. She knew it would be impossible to get a decent room at that hour. "If you don't mind."

"Not at all," he said.

"I suppose I could stay the night. I promise, I will be out of your hair tomorrow."

"Grace," he started to say and then heard a knock on the front door followed by a hello.

"Ahh, Aunt Emily is here." He stood up and so did Grace.

Aunt Emily set her basket on the counter in the kitchen, kissed David on the cheek and said, "I'm sorry, I didn't realize you had company."

"Aunt Emily, this is Grace."

Graces eyes opened wide. She pointed to her and said, "You're Emily Marshall."

Aunt Emily smiled, gave her a hug and replied, "Around here, I'm just Aunt Emily." She winked, adding, "Thank you for recognizing me." She opened her basket and pulled out a bottle of Cabernet Sauvignon. "David, open this for me please." Then she looked at Grace and said, "Wait until you try the rhubarb Crostatas. David, I made a fresh raspberry cheesecake, by any chance do you have any vanilla ice cream?"

"When Aunt Emily says ice cream, she means homemade, not store bought," he said and raised his eyebrows at Grace.

"Yes, I do as a matter of fact." He set the wine and three glasses down on the table along with several dessert plates. "Let me grab the ice cream and then I will open the wine."

"Would you mind if I take a few pictures of your desserts?" Grace asked, holding up her cellphone. "My friends and I are huge fans of yours. We all follow you on Instagram."

"Of course, you may," Aunt Emily said as she set the silver server down next to the Crostatas.

David set the container of ice cream in the ice bucket and asked if Grace would like a picture of her with Aunt Emily.

Aunt Emily stood next to her with her arm around her and they both smiled for the camera.

David began to pour the wine. "Grace?"

"Please." She held her glass up.

Aunt Emily handed each of them a plate. "Grace, do you live nearby?"

Grace pulled the glass back from her mouth. "No, I'm from Connecticut. I was supposed to rent the house for the summer; however, we ran into a snag."

Aunt Emily snapped her neck back, "We?" looking over at David.

Grace answered her. "I made the mistake of renting David's house from someone who was not legitimate. David was kind enough to not throw me out and now he's trying to help me find the man who did this to me."

"Someone rented your house without you knowing?" Aunt Emily said and then picked up her glass of wine. "Well, let's toast to the smart bastard."

"Yeah, except I guess he didn't count on me being here for the summer," David said.

"He? Do you know his name? Who does he work for?" Aunt Emily asked. She couldn't imagine her nephew allowing any of this to go on.

"Grace and I are not sure if he is legit. He probably works for himself."

"I found the house on Google. Beach house for rent by owner," she said adding, "the ad said it was a summer only rental. I was shocked it was even available."

"Do I dare ask how much?" Aunt Emily asked as she set slices of Crostatas on everyone's plate.

David looked at Grace waiting for her to answer. When she hesitated, he said, "I told Grace she can stay here for the summer and I'll go to the--"

"No," Grace said. "I will not allow that. This is totally my fault." She shook her head. "David, this is your home. I appreciate the offer, but I'll figure something out." Then she looked at Aunt Emily and said, "Twenty-seven-thousand dollars for the summer."

"Good Lord!" Aunt Emily cried. "Grace, my house is empty for the weekend. You're more than welcome to stay there until you find the rat bastard who did this to you." She raised her hand. "I won't take no for an answer. You'll have the entire guest wing to yourself."

Grace knew exactly where her house was. She's seen the main rooms, every garden and the magnificent views of the ocean. A breeze brushed by her and something inside told her to stay at David's. He seemed genuine and he didn't mind having her around. Grace looked over at David. "If you are serious about my staying until we catch the man who took my money, I would like to stay here. If that's okay?"

Chapter Twenty

Aunt Emily kissed both of them goodbye and told Grace she was happy she decided to stay at David's. "He's a good man. He'll take good care of you and make sure you get your money back."

Grace touched Aunt Emily's elbow. "It was a pleasure meeting you. I'll be sure to share my photos on Instagram giving you rave reviews."

After Aunt Emily left, Grace said she was tired and needed to get some sleep. "All that walking tired me out." She held her hand up like a stop sign. "Before I even think about closing my eyes, I have to call my friends and let them know I met their idol."

David closed the front door and told Grace, "You can have the first guest room on the right."

She came to a sudden stop. "My bag is in my car."

David smiled. "I'll walk with you to get your car. You can park it in the driveway."

They went out the front door and headed down the sidewalk. "Hey, wait, it's your first day in Point Judith. You need to see the ocean at night, feel the cool sand under your feet and bask in the moon's glow." He headed toward the back of the house and she graciously followed him.

When she saw the moon's reflection on the water, it took her breath away. "The moon is so big," she said as she inhaled the cool crisp air. Her heart leveled as she picked up her pace to follow David in the dark. When they reached the jetty, they turned to the right along the wild rose bushes toward her car. She pointed and said, "Over there, the white Volvo."

They walked past crowds coming and going from local venues, they could hear laughter coming from the restaurants. People were sitting outside under patio lights at Chaplin's Seafood and on George's of Galilee's topside deck.

"There's so much to do here," she said as soon as she saw two men playing guitars outside a restaurant.

"Yeah, the streets don't close up until well after midnight. On the weekends you can hear their music from the back deck."

To the right three leggy women, all wearing miniskirts, arms laced together, swaying as they made their way out of the George's of Galilee Restaurant. Grace smiled as they walked past her. She knew the feeling of sisterhood. She had two best friends that would do anything for her. As Grace kept moving toward her car, she noticed David slowed his pace down. Grace looked to her left to see what David was looking at. Remarkably, he was not looking at the women, he was watching a man pick up what appeared to be a sandwich someone had tossed on the ground near a large blue dumpster. "Is he homeless?" She asked.

"Wait here," David told her.

She saw David take his wallet out of his back pocket. David walked up to the man and offered him some money. Grace heard the man tell David he never accepted charity in the past and he wasn't about to start now.

"My name is David. What's your name?"

"I know who you are Mr. Wayne," the man replied.

Grace moved closer to where they were.

"Listen, she already tried to toss me out of the house once today. If you don't take the money, she'll change the locks on the door and won't let me in." Once again, David held the money out to the gentleman. "Please," he said as he extended his hand to him.

"Everyone calls me Red," he said and shook his head. "I'm sorry, but you'll just have to sleep under the stars tonight. I can't accept your money."

Grace thought about what Hudson would do in a situation like this. She laced her arm through David's and said, "Red, it's nice to meet you. I'm Grace." She held her hand out to him. When he accepted her hand, she told him they all have something in common. "Everyone has a birthday, right?"

"Yes, Ma'am," Red replied.

"Red, I want you to do me a favor. Accept David's gesture as a birthday gift and when you buy yourself whatever your heart desires think of us as a couple of nice human beings living in this often-cruel world." She winked. "Or, he will be sleeping under the stars tonight."

David put the money in his hand. Grace leaned in and kissed Red on the cheek and whispered, "Happy birthday, handsome."

Red was a good-looking man in his late forties. Bright red hair, mustache and beard with the darkest brown eyes Grace had ever seen. "Bless your hearts," Red said as he handed the money back to David. "I don't need your money. Promise me, you will always take care of each other." Then he looked at Grace and said, "Don't ever let go of him."

Grace became emotional.

David shook his hand and told him it was nice to have met him. Grace whispered goodbye, as she and David walked to her car. Red touched her heart in a way she could not explain. She never took back her arm until David opened the car door for her. He walked around to the passenger side, got in and noticed a photo of a man on her dashboard. "He's good looking."

Grace felt a lump in her throat. She didn't respond to David's comment because she didn't know how. She pressed the ignition button and backed out of the parking lot.

David sensed she was uncomfortable and changed the sub-ject telling her to stay to the right at the roundabout toward Sand Hill Cove. "The first driveway on the right," he said.

"One of the things I liked most about your place was that it is within walking distance to everything and you had the biggest parcel of land. All the other houses are so close together."

"My father was smart and bought three lots."

"You must be inundated with offers," she said as she turned into his driveway.

"Not so much anymore," he replied. He opened his door and told her he would carry her bags inside. When he reached the front door, he put one bag down to open the door for her. Then he headed for the guest room with the full bathroom. "You should be comfortable in here. If you need anything, let me know." He set her bags down on the bench at the foot of the bed. "I go jogging at five every morning, you're welcome to join me."

She smiled. "I think I'll sleep in tomorrow morning, but perhaps one day." She put her pocketbook down and thanked him again for his hospitality. "I can't thank you enough."

"Stop, it's not your fault." He turned to leave, but turned around to tell her. "Maria will be here on Monday. If you want anything special to eat or drink, there's a list on the cork board in the kitchen just write it down and she will bring it back when she comes on Wednesday."

She looked at him puzzled. "Maria? You never mentioned your wife was coming home."

"I'm sorry. Maria's my house manager. She does my laundry, cleans, shops and keeps me organized."

Grace let out a breath and grinned. "Gotcha. Hey, that was a very nice thing you did tonight."

"It broke my heart watching him eat from a dumpster. To think he gets his meals from a garbage can makes me sick." David shook his head. "I don't think I have ever met a man with more pride than him. I respect him. Not happy about his lifestyle, but I respect him for not taking handouts. I seriously thought you had him when you said it was for his birthday."

Grace smiled. "I tried," she said and then told him, "He didn't eat the garbage, he tossed it in the dumpster. Good night, David." She was dying to call Ella and Ava. She went into the bathroom to change and noticed it was stocked with the same Mrs. Meyer's soaps, lotions and guest towels as the half bathroom down the hall. Leaving only her underwear on she tossed on a clean tank top and headed for the bed. She wanted to call them but she was not sure how close David's bedroom was, so she texted them. "Hey, you are not going to believe who I met tonight."

"Grace!" Ava texted.

"Who?" Ella wrote.

"Emily Marshall," Grace replied smiling from ear to ear knowing they would both kill to meet her in person.

"Where?" Ella asked.

"Here, at the house, she's, his aunt." Grace wrote and then proceeded to tell them both everything that'd happened with the listing agent. "I'm going to stay here and hopefully catch him, get my money back and then go to a hotel."

"Wait. So, the owner is still at the house?" Ava texted.

"Yes, David lives here. What was I supposed to do? Throw him out of his own house?"

"Grace?" Ella wrote followed by, "Oh my goodness! You know who he is right?" She sent Grace a picture of David.

"Shut the front door!" Ava wrote.

Grace looked at the photo, read the caption and texted back. "I never would have guessed. He's so nice, genuine and kind."

Ella sent another photo to Grace. That one showed David on the cover of Forbes Magazine. "Billionaire, David Wayne shares his secrets on banking in today's busy times."

Ava wrote, "Forget about him, I want to meet Emily!"

Grace sent photos of the desserts Emily served earlier and said she would call them first thing in the morning. "I'll call you tomorrow when I go for a walk on the beach so we can talk. I love and miss you both so much. Good night," she typed and whispered before setting her phone down on the nightstand.

Grace turned out the light and whispered, "Good night, my love." Then she looked out the window hoping he was watching over her. "I miss you so much." She turned to her side and closed her eyes.

Friday morning, Grace woke up to an empty house. David left a note on the cork board. "Enjoy your stay, I'll be back around seven. I'll bring lobster and prime rib." She saw where he had written be home, but erased it and wrote the word back.

She knew he was being cautious with her and she appreciated that. Especially, because she was already feeling awkward about being in his home. She spent the day walking on the beach, reading and every now and then crying for the love she lost. When she called Ella, she told her about meeting Red and how she couldn't get him to accept David's money. Grace was fine until Ella asked her how she was holding up. "I know you're hurting. I can hear it in your voice. I wish you stayed at my place." Ella started to cry and Grace lost it.

"I miss him so much. I can't believe he is gone. I keep checking my phone hoping he would call me. I keep thinking this is all a nightmare and when I wake up, he'll be standing at the altar giving me that gorgeous smile of his." Grace let out a scream. "Why? Why, Ella? I don't understand how any of this could happen, he was such a good person. Hudson longed to take care of people. He was good to everyone, why did they do this to him?"

Ella stopped breathing for a minute as she listened to Grace cry. "I don't know," she said. "I'm sorry it happened to you. I wish you were here so I could take care of you."

Grace paused swallowing back a sob. She never needed anyone to take care of her. All she ever wanted was someone to love her, raise amazing children and share a life together. "Sometimes, when I feel like my insides are going to burst, I can feel Hudson's hand on my shoulder." She shook her shoulders remembering each time. "I know he is with me. Ella, please try to understand I just need a little time to figure it all out. I can't go to work. I can't even walk down Main Street without someone asking me if I am okay. I don't want to see people right now." She laughed through her crying tears. "I'm right where I am supposed to be."

"I love you," Ella cried into the phone.

"I love you more," Grace said and ended the call.

Grace thought about the eighteenth, knowing it would have been their wedding day. She looked up and whispered, "Please stay with me. Get me through one more day and I promise you I will become a stronger person."

At precisely seven o'clock, David walked in, held up a bag and said, "I hope you are hungry."

Grace smiled and offered to help. "Can I assist you?"

"Sure," he replied and set the bag on the counter. "Do you want to grill or boil the lobsters?"

She shrugged her shoulders. "Grilling is fine with me."

"Great," he said as he reached for the butter and herbs. "How was your day?"

Grace froze. It felt too much like being a couple. Him asking her how her day was. As much as she needed to be alone, to mourn the loss of Hudson, she felt safe with David and yet she didn't want to answer him. She didn't want any of this to feel right. She simply said, "My friends were so excited to hear I got to meet Emily Marshall."

Chapter Twenty-One

A week later, David decided to give Grace the space she deserved. After all, she paid good money for the house. She wanted her privacy for a reason and they still hadn't heard any news about the guy who ripped her off. Every morning, while he went jogging, she remained in her room. It did not surprise him when she decided not to join him, she had been extremely quiet all week. She even ate her breakfast alone. During the day, she would sit on the beach and read, only once did he catch her doing yoga. David tried to give her more space by reading reports from engineers, the building department and from his legal team in his study. One day, he left a note saying he would be at the town hall all day. He had hoped she would take advantage of being alone in the house and feel comfortable enough to enjoy it. When he got home that evening, she was in her room, crying. David stood outside her door feeling terrible about not being able to help her or make her pain go away.

The next day, Grace was in the kitchen eating a tuna sandwich when David asked her, "Grace, would you be willing to go for a ride with me this afternoon?"

She thought about his generosity and felt compelled to oblige. "Sure," she replied.

"Great, we'll go after lunch if that's okay with you?"

Grace took her last bite and stood up. "Let me load the dishwasher and grab my pocketbook."

She went to pick up his plate, but when he tilted his head, she simply smiled and said, "Fine, just be sure to stack it correctly."

They both laughed.

David set his plate behind hers and closed the door to the dishwasher.

When they went outside Maria was pulling into the driveway. She got out and said, "Hello, Mr. David." Then she stuck her hand out to Grace. "Miss Grace, it is nice to see you again."

"The pleasure is all mine," Grace replied. "Oh, and thank you so much for picking up my coconut water."

"You need anything else, you let me know," she said and waved them off.

Grace got in David's car and said, "Your housekeeper is so nice. Let me get this straight, she drives a BMW and you drive a Tahoe?"

David backed out of the driveway. "I was lucky to obtain her services. All of her other clients are celebs on Watch Hill."

"Like Aunt Emily and Taylor Swift," Grace said as she latched her seat belt.

"Grace, I want you to be comfortable at the beach house."

"David, I assure you. I'm quite comfortable and it really doesn't bother me that you are there."

He bobbed his head several times, snapped his neck, focused on the road and drove in silence wondering if she meant it or if she was just trying to make him feel better about intruding in on her vacation because it seemed to him like she was avoiding him whenever she had the chance. That morning, he was standing in the tower, looking down at the beach and saw her crying. It seemed she went through an entire box of tissues. That bothered him. Seeing her like that, he could only assume the man in the photo left her for another woman or left her at the altar. Whatever the reason, she deserved her time alone to figure it all out.

When he turned off the main road and pressed the keypad opening the large black iron gate, she asked him, "Where are we going?"

"I want to show you, my cabin."

She looked at him. The cabin was less than an hour away from the beach house. Unlike his ocean front property this was in a secluded area. "Is that your cabin?" She asked pointing to the gatehouse.

"No, a friend of mine lives there. He takes care of the place and keeps me supplied with firewood."

David drove up the long, private driveway until he reached a massive log cabin.

Grace looked at him. "You have got to be kidding?"

David chuckled. "I built it a few years ago. It's my quiet nest. I come here, to get away from the crowds." When she got out of the Tahoe, David gave her a moment to take it all in. The scenery took her breath away, green lawns overlooking a manmade pond and what promised to be the most spectacular sunsets in Rhode Island. "Come on, I'll show the inside." He opened the front door for her to enter the foyer.

"Oh, wow, I feel like I am standing inside a Cabela's store." She touched the hand carved thick wood on the railing. "David, this staircase is gorgeous." Grace walked over to the massive stone fireplace and noticed she could see directly into the other room.

"That's my study," he said and then asked if she wanted something to drink. "Sparkling water, wine, beer?"

"I'll have whatever you are having," she replied and stepped back to look out the window. "The back yard is even more amazing than the front," she said.

David handed her a Michelob and a glass. She smiled, took a sip from the bottle and said, "Thank you."

He smiled back at her and set the glass down. "Grace, you are something else. Let's sit out back, drink our beer and then I'll show you the rest of the place."

Grace followed him outside where she was once again in awe. She smiled seeing the enormous outdoor kitchen, swimming pool, hot tub and what appeared to be a hiking trail leading into the woods.

"I brought you up here so you could see for yourself that you are not putting me out of my home. I've decided to spend the rest of the summer up here." He raised his hand. "I will not take no for answer. You deserve your privacy. I overheard you telling your friends you were sorry they couldn't visit as planned."

Grace set her empty bottle on the table. "David, I was just going to ask you how you felt about living in the house with three single women for a weekend." She shook her head. "Ella and Ava wanted to visit for a week, but their helper, Olivia had a change of plans, so they can only come for the weekend. Trust me, they want to meet you. Okay," she laughed. "Actually, they want to meet Aunt Emily and if you're not home, she won't stop by." Grace picked up her bottle and said, "Bartender, I'll have another and umm, I'd like to see the rest of the place."

David laughed, reached out his hand and said, "Right this way." They stopped in the kitchen, grabbed two more beers and walked through the cabin. "I toured a few log cabins while I was in Montana and in Switzerland. I have to say none of them compared to the cabin I visited in Marquette, Michigan. It was massive. A twenty-six-thousand-square foot man cave."

"Wow. How many rooms were there?" Grace asked as she entered the first bedroom.

"Fifty, I believe," David said standing in the doorway. "This is the bears den."

She laughed, "I can see that." From the quilt to the drapes to the leather chair's throw blanket, bear prints were everywhere. "I actually like the design. Pine trees and black bears." She picked up the soft needlepoint pillow, inhaling the same scent as her bathroom at the beach house. "Ahh, rain water. Right?"

David nodded. Pointed his finger at her and said, "It was better than Lemon Verbena, Lavender, or some other flowery scent. I hope you like wild animals," he said as she stepped into the next guest bedroom containing white tailed deer on the curtains, bedspread and toss pillows.

They walked back downstairs and then down the hall leading to a large bedroom and den area. "This is my private quarters," he said.

She turned around and said, "No animal prints?"

He laughed. "Sorry, I like monochromatic."

She walked over to the fireplace. "This is gorgeous."

"I purposely designed the house so my guest have their own living space and they are far enough away from my room to give me the right amount of privacy."

She nodded. "Well, I love it." David's room was designed in shades of ivory, cream and stark white. "I like the open floor plan." She said as she entered the living room. "How big is the cabin?"

"Eighty by forty," he replied. "Grace, if you ever want to be alone, I don't mind the drive."

As they made their way to the living room David explained he was only trying to give her the privacy she paid for. "You said it yourself you needed to be alone."

Grace thought for a moment. "David, having you stay at the beach house is far from me living in my home town. I couldn't even go into a grocery store without someone asking me how I was holding up or having a stranger walk up to me and tell me how sorry they were. I appreciate what you are trying to do here, but you don't have to leave. You can stop trying to make me feel better. If you truly want to help me, live your life as if I am not there."

David nodded approvingly. "You got it!" Then he extended his hand and offered to show her the game room. "Have you ever played pool?"

She followed him down the hall. On the left was a half bathroom, gorgeous wood paneling and an enormous room filled with burgundy leather furniture and yes, a pool table. "I have and I have to tell you I am pretty good." She walked up to the table, brushed her hand along the top rail and asked him if he was any good. "Are you a cunning player?" She raised her brows waiting for his answer.

He laughed. "I can hold my own."

Chapter
Twenty-Two

David sat on the guardrail near the side of the road, waiting and watching as people boarded various fishing boats. Cars pulled in from Great Island Road and Galilee Escape Road. He spotted a new fishing boat, Fishing Machine Charters out on the water and wondered if they arrived before the inn closed its doors? The old timers: Seven B's, Frances Fleet and Pamela May Charters were strong diehard fishing boats, strong enough to survive bad weather, a bad economy and hopefully a shattered inn.

Cars coming and going had license plates from at least a dozen different states. He couldn't help but wonder where everyone was staying. The old inn tugged at his heart. Memories of his father teaching him to swim. Sitting by the pool listening to the men and women talk about their day out on the ocean.

"David?" Someone asked. "It that you?"

David turned around and saw a familiar face. "Russ, hey how are you?" The two men shook hands. Russ Benn is the owner of the Seven B's custom fishing vessel. Russ was the man who taught David how to cast in rocky water.

"It's nice to see you," David said. "How's business?"

"It's been good to me, I can't complain. I've been a captain now for forty-nine years. I still love greeting every one of my passengers. I welcome back a lot of friendly faces from time to time. Congratulations on all your success," Russ said and held his hand out again.

David shook his hand and thanked him. "Thank you."

"When did you get back?"

"A few weeks ago," he replied. "Can I ask you something?"

Russ nodded. "Anything," he said and then crossed his arms.

"Did your business get hurt when the inn shut down?"

Russ uncrossed his arms and threw them in the air. "We all felt it. As you can imagine the first question they ask when they book a trip is where is the closest lodging." Russ shook his head. "It's a shame that bastard walked away like he did. The Lighthouse Inn was the only affordable solution for our guests." He tilted his head. "Are you?"

David nodded. "I'm going to try my best to see what I can do. I'd like to rebuild the inn. If the town will allow it. It seems like I have to go through a lot of hoops first."

"I hear you. We had a meeting to see if we could buy it, but there were just too many regulations, demands and bullshit to deal with for me. Thirty-two of us got together. We were willing to buy the place, fix it up and open it back up to the public, but the town wanted us to pay for and have an asbestos assessment performed. As soon as we agreed to do that, they told us we needed to file for a center for disease control permit. That's when we walked away. It didn't have to come to that. We offered to buy the inn six months after he closed the doors. Now look at the place. What used to be a sweet spot in Point Judith is a contractor's worst nightmare."

David took in deep breath before saying, "I promise you, all of you. I will give it my best shot."

Russ reached out and hugged David. "Thank you. Hey, it's nice to have you back home again. You're welcome to come fishing day or night."

David shook his hand and said he would like that. When he got home, Grace was sitting in a lounge chair with a shade umbrella behind her. Her book and YETI bottle lying next to what appeared to be her lunch, still in its container. David cleared his throat. "May I join you?"

Grace turned, blocking the sun with her hand. "Of course."

It was two in the afternoon and the sun was high above them. David sat on the beach, legs stretched out, leaning back on his hands. "Would you like to go deep sea fishing with me next week?"

Grace held her hand to her chin, tilted her head and said, "I have never been. I suppose I could try it. Do I need to do anything special to prepare for it?"

David grinned. "Sneakers or boat shoes, jeans and Dramamine a few hours before should do it."

Grace laughed. "Can I wear a tee shirt to prevent sun burn?"

David sat up, shook his finger at her and told her she was funny. "Yes, and sun block. I saw an old friend of mine and he invited me to go fishing for the day. It's an eighty-foot family-owned fishing vessel owned by my friend, Russ. Have you ever eaten Fluke?"

Grace shook her head. "I don't think so, but I love fish"

"Well, the best time to catch them is during the months of May and June. So, the timing is right and they taste amazing cooked on the grill."

Grace asked David if he had lunch yet. "I bought a salad big enough for four. Would you like to share it with me?"

David got up and said, "Yes, that sounds good. Let me grab something to drink and I will be right back."

Grace Googled deep sea fishing and read where they should pack a cooler with ice and bring their own drinks and food. When David returned Grace asked him how long will they be out on the water. "Will we be fishing long enough for me to pack a picnic basket?"

David sat next to her and told her they will board at seven in the morning and be out until around four in the afternoon. "Yes," he said adding, "but I have learned not to bring anything that requires mayonnaise." He laughed. "There isn't enough ice to keep that condiment cold."

David took hold of his salad telling Grace, "Russ Benn is an all-around nice guy. He started fishing charter tours as early as nineteen-sixty-two I believe. He made sure his fishing trips were affordable for singles and families alike."

There was something about David that she liked beyond his looks was his bona fide sincerity to everyone around him.

After they ate, Grace reached down, opened the small brown bag and took out two brownies. When she handed David one, he smiled knowing she waited for him to return before eating her lunch. "Thank you. Lunch was great."

"You're welcome," she said and closed her eyes as the sun had moved up from her legs to her face.

David made a mental note to order a beach umbrella for her. He saw a nice six foot by six down on the beach earlier in the week that would be perfect for her to read and enjoy her lunch under. Not to embarrass her, he would put it up without saying a word.

He had a lot to do before the next town meeting and he wanted to remain respectful of Grace's privacy. He stood up and said he had some calls to make. Then he reminded her that Aunt Emily would be stopping by later to drop off food. "Aunt Emily made you something special for tonight's dinner, so I hope you're not too full from lunch."

She laughed. "A grilled chicken salad would never stop me from eating Aunt Emily's delicious food."

Six o'clock, Aunt Emily arrived with not one but two picnic baskets. "Hellooo," she hollered as she came in the front door.

Grace had changed into a long flowing summer dress, wrapped her hair up in a ponytail, greeted Aunt Emily in the kitchen with a smile on her face and no shoes on her feet. "David," she called out. "Aunt Emily is here." Then she hugged her before taking one of the baskets. "It is nice to see you."

"Hello my dear. Any news on that awful person who took your money?"

"No not yet," Grace replied.

David entered the kitchen and gave his aunt a hug, kiss on the cheek and told her he was working on it. "We'll catch him. Don't you worry about that. Something smells good."

"Here, let's start with a cocktail. I made watermelon cosmos." Then she set a bowl of guacamole on the counter, shrimp and swordfish curry, along with basmati rice. "Oh, I want you to try a new dish." She took out a ceramic dish with Coffee Granita. "I also made a batch of shortbread cookies for dessert."

David reached in and set a short glass filled with Dahlias on the table. "This smell wonderful," he said as he lifted the glass for Grace to whiff.

"I love the smell of Dahlias right after you cut them," Aunt Emily said as she reached for three plates. "Shall we eat in the living room or take our plates out onto the back deck?"

"Can I take pictures first?" Grace said holding her cellphone in her hand. "Ella and Ava will shoot me if I don't share all of this with them."

Aunt Emily laughed aloud. "When are they coming?" She turned to face Grace. "They're coming right?"

"Yes, Fourth-of-July weekend," Grace replied. "David offered his guest rooms."

Aunt Emily winked at David. "You never stop amazing me." Then she put a piece of swordfish on her plate and went outside. They spoke about David taking Grace deep sea fishing for the first time and yes, he would make sure she took enough medicine to prevent her from getting sea sick.

After dinner, Aunt Emily said she had to leave early. "No time for dessert, I must be going. Enjoy!"

The following Wednesday, David and Grace each took Dramamine before they went to bed. And when they got up at five in the morning, they took another dose. They packed their picnic basket together, David tossed in plenty of Mosh Bars, bottled water and Aunt Emily's homemade blueberry muffins for the entire crew. Grace added a Caprese salad for two, cold pasta salad with fresh cherry tomatoes and basil along with six hard boiled eggs, apples and figs to snack on.

The captain personally welcomed them aboard. David shook his hand with one hand and handed his first mate the box filled with cookies. "Aunt Emily sends her love. Russ Benn, this is Grace. She's renting my beach house for the summer."

Grace shook his hand and said, "Thank you for the invitation. This is my first time."

"We'll take good care of you. Did you take your Dramamine?"

"Yes," she said laughingly.

"Then you will be fine. You've never seen a sun rise or set like the one you will see out on the ocean. Promise me you will both come back and take our sunset cruise."

That day, both Grace and David caught fish. Grace caught a Fluke while David caught several porgies. Grace promised the captain she would return. "I have to bring my friends, Ella and Ava." She winked at him. "Trust me, your first mate will love Ava."

Later, David offered to take Grace out for dinner, but she was too tired and scrambled eggs for them to eat out on the back deck. "I could sit here forever," she said as the sun began to set. "I am so glad I chose Salty Brine Beach."

David pursed his bottom lip, tilted his head and said, "Maybe, Point Judith...chose you."

"I think so," she said and took hold of their plates. "I'll grab us a cocktail." She came back out holding two glasses of Pinot Grigio. "It goes perfectly with eggs," she said and sat back down.

Chapter Twenty-Three

David attended every town meeting, was willing to meet all their requirements and yet he felt as if he was still up against a wall. "What more do I have to do to prove to you that I will satisfy every one of your demands?"

"Mr. Wayne, do you have thirty-million dollars to spend, because as it stands right now, we have a buyer willing to invest the money necessary to rebuild."

Another member interrupted him by saying, "No one wants a factory in the middle of tourist row."

David looked down at his notes. Nowhere in the last report did it mention another buyer willing to spend that kind of money or anything about a factory. "What kind of factory?" He asked.

The staunch old man replied, "A seafood processing facility along with the proper apparatus to purify the recycled water."

David felt defeated. The town was indeed a fishing mecca. A processing facility could work. "But what about the folks who want a decent place to stay?"

"A long day fishing? You have mentioned that a thousand times. We understand your desire to help the fishing community, but we have to be real. That building has to come down. This is the only solution."

David did not mean to yell however the old man was getting on his last nerve. "Because you allowed it to get this far. You should have allowed the fishing boat owners to buy the property years ago. Now, you want to abandon them. They need affordable lodging for their anglers."

"Are you willing to allow the hazmat team to give you a full assessment and pay whatever it takes to ensure the property is up to our specifications?"

"Yes!" David yelled. Then he held up the town's proposal. "What more do you want? Whatever it is, I want it in writing." David shook his head as he lowered his voice. "Please, just tell me what you want, and stop adding to the list every time I meet your demands." He stormed out the door before anyone had a chance to say anything. David was not happy with the town dragging their feet. As soon as he got in the car, he saw Aunt Emily had left a message on his cellphone. "Call me as soon as you get this message. I've uncovered something that I think might help you in your fight to save the inn."

"Hey," he said. "Old man Riggers needs to retire."

"Hmm, I was going to ask how the meeting went, but I see you met your nemesis."

David was in no mood for guessing games. His head was splitting and he hadn't eaten all day. "What are you trying to say?" He asked. "Did you find anything out on your end?"

Aunt Emily chuckled. "When you didn't call me right back, I sent you a fax. Read it and let me know how you want to proceed. By the way, I already called Helen and told her I would not be doing any more fundraisers for the town until she makes this right."

"You called the council president? Thank you," he said as he turned into his driveway. "What did she say?" He turned the engine off, sat back and listened as Aunt Emily explained.

"I think Rigger is getting a little kick back. Go read your fax and call me after you get something to eat." She always knows when he skips a meal.

"I'm sorry I was cranky," he said knowing he was a tad rude.

"David, before you go any news on Grace's money?"

"I haven't called in a few days. I'll look into it as soon as I figure out what the hell is going on with the inn."

Aunt Emily knew he was content having Grace at the beach house and she was glad Grace felt comfortable enough to stay in a man's home. They were good for each other and right now both Grace and the inn gave David good reason to stay at the beach house.

When David got out of the car, he realized Grace's car was not in the driveway. He went inside took one Advil and one

Tylenol, ate a tomato sandwich and read his email. Aunt Emily was correct. Old man Rigger and the investor were longtime friends. "Holy Crap!" David yelled as he read page two. Riggers had been accused of taking kickbacks when he was on the town council board in Providence.

"David? Are you okay?" Grace called out to him from the bottom of the staircase.

He went downstairs and explained everything and said how horrible it would be if he did not get the inn. "I have to figure out a way to get around all the bureaucratic inefficiencies." Then he saw a piece of sea glass on the counter next to her pocketbook. "That's nice," he said pointing to the blue stone.

"Beautiful, right?" Grace said. "I wish I had found another one. I would like to give them to Ella and Ava."

Taking a walk was the perfect solution for David. He needed to release the stress building up inside and hammering his muscles. "I can take you if you would like?"

David took hold of his cellphone and looked up when the next low tide would happen. "Perfect, by the time we get there we should be able to find a ton of sea glass." He explained the best time to find sea glass was when the tide was out. "Just south of the clam shack there is a mile walk full of gems."

"Great, let me change into shorts and I'll meet you on the beach," she replied.

David waited for her near the Adirondack chairs. First, he stretched out his arms, legs and then his back trying to release the tension from building up any more than it already had.

Grace came down the stairs wearing a pair of cutoff blue jeans and white V-neck tee shirt. David rolled up the cuffs of his jeans, kicked off his boat shoes and waved to her to follow.

As soon as she stepped out onto the beach, she saw the beach umbrella. He smiled and waved for her to follow him.

"Thank you," she whispered.

"You're welcome," he whispered back to her.

"How is sea glass formed?" She asked after nudging him on his elbow.

"Over many years; the salt water and sand churn the recycled glass until it is smooth enough to hold in your hands."

"So does it come in a variety of colors?"

David thought for a second. "The real stuff mostly comes in shades of blue."

As soon as the tide went out, they saw turquoise, sky blue, ice blue and aquamarine. Grace ran to pick up a few of the stones. "These are absolutely gorgeous."

Chapter Twenty-Four

Tuesday, no one thought to take anything out for dinner. The weather was perfect for dining outside. David knew he had to tread lightly with Grace. She kept her distance a well-known fact. Whenever he was downstairs, she made an excuse to be outside or in her room. He overheard her telling one of her friends that she was not ready for a relationship nor was she looking to have one with her house partner. *Jilted lover,* he thought. Husband ran off with her best friend perhaps. All he knew was he was hungry and he did not want to be rude and leave her hanging. "Grace, I was about to go to The Coast Guard House and grab a bite to eat, you're welcome to join me."

She looked up at the clock. Dinner sounded good.

Silence for what seemed forever before she stood up and said, "Sure, why not. But I am buying."

"Not a chance," he said. "First, let's get your money back then you can buy me dinner for making me stick around with all these people on my beach."

She shook her head. "Fine. Do I have to change?"

He looked at her. She was wearing a striped shirt, white clam diggers and a pair of sparkling blue and silver sandals. "Nope, you're fine, but let me put on a pair of clean shorts."

They sat out on the back deck overlooking the ocean. The warm breeze was the perfect medicine for David's head, back and nerves. "Do you like oysters?" He asked and she told him yes.

When their server came over to the table and asked for their drink orders, David ordered the ice crusher for them to split. "Grace what would you like to drink?"

She looked at the woman and asked what the house special was. The woman replied, "The chocolate cosmo is to die for."

"Great, I'll have two. He's buying."

David laughed, "Give the lady what she wants."

"I'm kidding. I'll try the cosmo and a glass of water, with lemon and no ice please."

David ordered a beer and asked if they could have a few minutes to read the menu.

"Absolutely, I'll be right back with your drinks."

"Ooo, twelve oysters, littleneck clams and shrimp. Great starter," Grace said. "I think I will have the Branzino then."

"You're going to love it. The chef prepares it to perfection. I am going to go with the seared scallops and a side of Brussel sprouts with smoked bacon and raisins."

The server came back with their drinks and took their orders.

"Can I ask you a question?" Before lifting her glass to take a sip.

"Anything," he replied and sat back in his chair feeling more relaxed than he had all week.

"Where do you go during the day?"

"To the town hall, to see my attorney, sometimes I go to the engineer's office and starting this week I will be meeting with an architect."

"Is there anything I can help you with?" She asked and took her first sip. "Oh, my goodness, this is amazing." She held the glass out for him to take a sip. "You have to try it."

He laughed out loud. "Sorry, I didn't mean to laugh, but it's my concoction. I dated the bartender the summer after we graduated high school. She loved anything that had chocolate in it."

"Have you had many girlfriends? No, wait," she said and shook her head. "It's none of my business. I'm sorry."

He drank from his beer and pointed the bottle toward her. "I said anything." He cleared his throat. "Would you consider six a lot?"

Her face was no longer red. "No," she replied and emptied her glass. "Have you ever been in love?"

"Once," he said. Raised his hand for their server to come back to the table. "Grace, would you care for another cocktail?"

"No, thank you," she replied and took a sip of her water. "I'm good."

"I'll have another beer when you bring out our dinner."

"You got it."

"My high school sweetheart. I went away to college. I guess she couldn't wait four years. By the time I came home she was already married and had a couple of kids." He tilted his head and raised his hand as if to say oh well. "So, I went to California and studied finance."

Grace thought for a moment before saying, "Losing someone you love hurts."

"Yes, it does," he replied as their server set the starter filled with delicious appetizers down on the table. "Grace." He held his hand out for her to go first.

After they ate, David told Grace about growing up with his aunt and how he couldn't say Emily. "I called her Auntie M until I was five or six. Can you imagine a woman who used to declare she never wanted to have children because she was going to travel around the world, to literally putting her life on hold to raise a teenage boy?"

"She is an amazing woman, a great role model for so many of us. Ava, Ella and I absolutely adore her."

"Living with Aunt Emily I had the best upbringing. Every day was a new adventure. She would take me digging for clams at the foot of Newport Pell Bridge in Jamestown's Potter Cove, in the Tiverton's Sapowet Marsh, and in Long Neck Cove in Portsmouth among many other places."

"I seriously believe in my heart that she doesn't regret giving up one day of traveling to be with you."

"Hmm, I hope you're right." After they ate, David asked if she wanted to go for a walk down the beach. "It's still light out. Care to walk off some of these calories?"

Grace was not surprised the evening went well. Still, she was struggling to fight back tears. She swallowed the lump in her throat, twirled her hair and said, "Sure, why not?"

David ran his hand through his lush hair when he noticed Grace blink away tears. "Yeah, a walk will do us both good." He got up as did Grace.

Grace slipped her sandals off and asked David to name a few places she should take Ella and Ava to see during their stay in Point Judith. "Any sightseeing suggestions for when Ella and Ava visit?"

"The Breakers is the largest and most magnificent of the Newport mansions. It's a seventy-room estate owned by the Vanderbilt family."

"Do you know how they made their money?"

"The Vanderbilt's built their empire in steamships and the New York Central Railroad."

"You know history," she said and bent down to pick up a sea shell. "Maybe, I will take them digging for clams one day."

"Not to intrude on your time with your friends, but if I go with you, you won't need a permit. Residents don't require a license to dig for clams only nonresidents. The fee is two-hundred dollars for the year."

"Seriously?" She looked at him. "You're just saying that because you want to spend time with us." She laughed so hard she made him laugh. "I'm kidding. When is the best time to go? In the morning or afternoon?"

David chuckled a little before telling her, "At low tide. In other words when there is more land than water."

"Now, you're just making fun of me." She slapped his shoulder. "I'm telling Aunt Emily."

Chapter
Twenty-Five

July 3rd was a sunny day. The water was warm and that meant the beaches were full of sun seekers.

Ella and Ava arrived at ten o'clock just as promised. They were ready to relax, hit the beach and meet their food goddess. Grace opened the front door the moment David called out to her from the kitchen. "Ella and Ava are here."

Grace came running in from the back deck. "Look at that they are right on time. That's a first!" She waved to them as they were getting out of their car.

David walked past her. "I'll help them with their luggage."

Ella got out of the car, stretched and headed for the backseat before she realized David was standing beside her. "Oh, gosh! Hey, how are you?" She said as she opened the car door.

"Here let me help you with that," he said smiling.

Ava raised her eyebrows before running up to see Grace. "I missed you so much. Please tell me you are okay."

Grace gave her a kiss on the cheek and told her she was fine.

"You always say that. You look great." Ava turned back around and pointed toward David and Ella. "He's hot. You know Ella has a crush on him."

"Ella has Melvin," Grace said before asking, "right?"

"No, I think they broke up. She said something about not being able to get him to stop working or talking about the--" Ava stopped herself from mentioning the legal case. Ella made her promise not to mention a word while they were there. She clapped her hands together. "Am I really going to get to meet Emily Marshall this weekend?"

Grace smiled. "Yes, Ava, you are."

"Yay, I even brought my Canon camera and ring light for taking pictures." Her hands went to her mouth. "Is she cooking for us? Can I take pictures?"

"She is the sweetest person you will ever meet and yes she is preparing something just for you and Ella."

David walked past them carrying five bags. "I think they're staying longer than they told you," he said laughingly. "I'll put them in their rooms."

Ava pointed to the bags. "Mine are the cute leopard prints."

"Ella told me," he replied and said, "I'm David, it's nice to meet you."

When Ella and Grace made eye contact, they both started to cry. Ella whispered in her ear, "I'm right here. I got you."

Ella wrapped her arms around Grace and after what seemed to be a long minute she stood back after Grace told her, "No crying." Grace wiped her own tears from her face. "Please, I've done enough crying this past month. I want the two of you to enjoy yourselves."

Ava gathered for a group hug and when she let out her loud cry, David came running back. "Is everyone okay?"

Ava's tears turned to laughter. "I get so emotional. I'm sorry. Thank you for taking care of Grace. Gosh, thanks for letting us stay here." She held out her hand and David took it in his own.

"You're welcome. By the way, Aunt Emily will be here first thing in the morning. She's excited to meet the two of you."

Grace felt a hand on the small of her back. "I'm going out for a while. The baskets are a nice touch," he whispered and then told everyone he would see them at dinner time. "Please feel free to use the house as if it were Grace's." He winked before turning to leave. David was going to the cabin to meet with his friend about the guy who stole Grace's money. He didn't tell her out of fear it was bad news. "Have fun," David shouted.

"Thank you," Grace said knowing he was giving her time to be alone with her best friends. Then she turned to Ella and Ava. "Wait until you meet Aunt Emily, she is above and beyond adorable. Emily and David have been planning a surprise since the day I told them the two of you were coming."

"Are we going to her house?" Ava asked.

"I'm not sure, all I know is you are going to love her." When she looked at Ella, she saw tears in her eyes. Grace shook her head. "Believe me, my heart is broken. He was the love of my life. Now, go change because we are going to relax on the beach and catch up on the two of you." Grace inhaled before pointing her finger at the two of them. "I'm going to change into my bathing suit. I'll meet you in the living room in ten minutes." When Grace entered her bedroom, she collapsed onto the bed, hugged a pillow and cried for Hudson one more time. Just seeing her friends and knowing they were supposed to be standing beside her at her wedding made her feel sad.

Both Ella and Ava noticed their welcome baskets filled with snacks, sun screen, beach towels, books and their own special piece of sea glass.

When Ava walked out wearing an orange bikini, Grace sucked in a breath. "Good Lord, Ava! How much weight have you lost in the past month?"

"I don't know," she replied as she wrapped a turquoise, orange and gold sarong around her waist.

Ella shook her head. "All she eats is a damn salad. Every day at three o'clock she eats a salad and drinks a vitamin water. That is it."

Grace looked at Ava with concern. "What is going on?"

Ava waved Ella off. "Salads are healthy. I make sure to add a protein. Have you ever eaten quinoa? It's so good. Wait until I make you my strawberry and spinach salad." Ava picked up her beach bag. "I add pecans as my protein."

Grace just looked at her. One thing was for sure, something was going on with Ava. "I have drinks and snacks for all of us."

Ava held up a bottle of Core water. "It has a cucumber essence. I love it."

"Trust me Grace, she is never hangry." Ella smiled. "Seriously, we both know she's in love again."

Grace turned around and said, "Do tell." Then she opened the gate leading down to the beach.

Ella walked down first followed by Ava and then Grace. Ava jokingly said, "Tell us about your man."

"David ... is not my anything!" Grace said loud enough for everyone on the beach to hear.

When Ella reached the bottom step, she let Ava go past her. She put her hand on Grace's shoulder. "She didn't mean it that way. She's just curious about his aunt. We all know what Hudson meant to you."

Ava turned to face them. "I'm sorry."

"Make no mistake I am not interested in David or any other man. My heart needs time to heal. Hudson and I had plans, we were getting ready to start a family. He was my heart and soul."

Ava's face turned red. She swallowed the lump in her throat before saying, "I'm so sorry. I didn't mean any disrespect. I know Hudson was your world. I was just curious about David's life, lifestyle and getting to meet his aunt."

Ella inhaled, looked at Grace and knew without a doubt she already forgave Ava because, well it was Ava.

Grace hugged Ava and told her she loved her. Then she told them both about a boutique on Succotash Road. "They have the cutest tops and sweaters with red lobsters on them."

"Can we walk there now," Ava asked adding, "I'm dying for some inspiration?"

Grace laughed. "Only if you can walk on water."

Ella pushed Ava to the side. "Can we please just spend a few minutes relaxing and not talk about clothes?"

"Fine," Ava replied. "Wait. What's the name of the place? I'll Google it."

"Pink Pineapple in Narragansett."

Grace set her bag down next to her chair, while Ella stuck her toes in the water. When she returned, she sat on the Adirondack chair to Grace's right. "This is amazing." She leaned back, exhaled and kicked off her flip flops.

Grace grabbed her book hoping to avoid any more comments or questions about David. "I have four more chapters to read." She held up "That's Outside My Boat" I want to know how it ends.

Ella opened her bag and took out one of the books Grace had given to her. "This looks interesting."

Ava was already making notes and scrolling on the boutique's website.

Grace noticed in the time it took her to read four chapters, Ava drank four bottles of water. When she offered Ava her favorite rice cake with peanut butter and blueberries on it, she knew Ava had a serious problem. Unlike Grace and Ella, Ava grew up in a stable home, she was emotionally and financially secure. Allowing her to feel comfortable in her own little world. Ella was an only child; her mother and father would have done anything for her. She didn't have as much as Ava, but she grew up in a loving home. Grace on the other hand, was on her own since she was sixteen, working full time while still attending high school.

Grace lifted her eyes above her book admiring her two friends. Two very different women who shared a passion for the same thing. She was grateful for them. She chuckled just thinking about how wild and crazy Ava can be and how spontaneous Ella can be when she's in the mood to let her hair down. She used to worry about Ella being so in-check about her business and its financial future. Many times, Grace tried to get Ella to get her real estate license, but each time Ella assured her, Ava needed her more.

A minute went by before Grace noticed Ella looking at a group of men playing volleyball.

"Now that looks like fun." Grace set her book down and tapped Ava on her leg.

"Wow," Ava said and stood up. "Come on." She waved to them and they both got up. The ladies sat at the only empty table on the beach. A minute later, a server came over to the table and asked what they wanted to drink.

"Three Coors Light," Ella said.

When the server came back with their second round, Grace asked for six dozen little neck clams. "Steamed, please."

"Sounds good, I'll bring a side of butter and cocktail sauce."

By the time the women were on their fifth round, their team had moved down the beach. Forcing the ladies to pick up their drinks and follow them. Four tables later and another round of beers, clams and a few dirty napkins their team had won the tournament.

"We better get back, take a nap and get dressed for dinner," Grace said.

"Where is David taking us?" Ella asked.

"Who cares," Ava responded. "We are on vacation."

Grace raised her eyebrows at Ella. When she put her arm around her, she whispered in her ear. "She ate more clams than the two of us together."

Ella laughed. "Umm, did Ava tell you about the flowers she received at work the other day?"

"I knew you were going to tell her," Ava said.

On the way back to David's beach house, Ava told Grace and Ella about the man she had been dating. "I've been seeing him for about three months. I don't understand him. He buys me nice things, tells me gorgeous al the time, but he never talks about our future. He's just funny that's all."

"What do you mean?" Grace asked.

"For instance, he bought me this bikini, right? I told him thank you when he gave it to me and yet when I climbed into the hot tub with him, he turned cold."

"Because you wore the suit in the hot tub? I don't understand," Grace said.

Ava pursed her lips. "I didn't wear anything. I got in naked, thinking I would say thank you by having sex with him in the hot tub."

"Oh, Ava! Have I not taught you anything?" Ella said and then told her, "You should have worn the bikini, stood in front of him and slowly took it off."

Ava scratched her head. "Screw that. This dating shit is for the birds. I am not working that hard to please any man."

"Huh," Grace said aloud. *That's why she's not eating?* "Ava, I hope you try something new tonight. The seafood is to die for. Everything is fresh and cooked to perfection."

"Don't worry, I'm done with Mr. My Way."

That night the ladies sat topside at George's of Galilee. Grace had never heard them laugh so hard or long. David had them in stitches. "So, I'm sitting in my chair and this crazy woman comes at me screaming I'm in her house. I immediately think she's on drugs."

Grace laughed aloud before telling David to stop exaggerating.

Chapter Twenty-Six

Ava was so excited she was up before anyone else. She made herself a cup of coffee, took it outside, sat on the deck and watched the sun rise. At six-thirty she saw David jogging toward the beach house. She waved to him, but he didn't notice her until she stood up. He motioned for her to come down to the beach. Ava stood in front of David until he spun her around in time to witness a line of sailboats leaving the Point Judith Harbor of Refuge. "Wow, that is cool. They are all so beautiful," she said and turned back around. "How was your jog?"

"Great," David replied. "I enjoy the cool air right before the sun starts to rise."

"It was magnificent this morning. I was so excited to meet your aunt I couldn't sleep."

David chuckled. "She's thrilled about meeting you and Ella. I heard she prepared a feast for you to sample today."

"Oh, trust me, I plan on eating whatever she makes," Ava said as she made her way up the stairs. When she reached the top step, she turned to face him and said, "Thanks again for having us." Then she opened the gate.

Grace was sitting in the living room with a cup of coffee and her cellphone. "Good morning, you two," she said as David and Ava came inside.

"Good morning," they both replied.

"Ava, coffee?" David asked as he headed to the kitchen.

"Sure, let me grab my cup." She went out onto the deck, grabbed her cup and met him in the kitchen. "Thank you."

David and Ava sat in the living room with Grace. "Ella is in the shower," Grace said. "I think she's excited to meet Aunt Emily."

"Me, too," Ava said before sipping her coffee. "I tossed and turned all night thinking about meeting her in person. Gosh, I hope I can contain myself." She looked at the clock and saw it was nearly seven thirty. "I better get ready. What are we supposed to wear?"

David set his cup down. "I would pack a bathing suit, that's for sure."

"Grace, what are you wearing?" Ava asked as she got up.

"I don't know. David, what are you wearing?" Grace laughed. "It's a girl thing. We have to know."

"Denim shorts, tee shirt and my boat shoes." He smiled wondering if either of them caught on to his hint. "Dress casual."

"Shorts it is," said Grace and Ava left the room running.

"I'll tell Ella," she said as she turned the corner down the hall.

Grace sat back, tucked her legs under her buttocks and asked David how his morning jog was. "How far did you run today?"

He pursed his lips. "About six miles," he replied and then finished his coffee. "Shower time or you ladies will wish you left me at home."

Grace picked up her book and read two chapters before Ella came out looking for another cup of coffee.

"We are going to have to tie her down soon. Ava is a crazy woman. She scared the crap out of me. I was in the damn shower and she banged on the glass, 'everyone is wearing sh orts.'" Ella shook her head. Filled her cup up and asked Grace, "Did you hear me?"

Grace laughed aloud. "Yes, she's been up all night. I hope she doesn't knock poor Aunt Emily over when she sees her."

Nine a.m., Aunt Emily pulled into David's driveway, tooting her horn for him to come out and help her load his Tahoe.

"Ava, Ella," David hollered. "Aunt Emily is here," he said as he opened the front door.

All three women came out to greet her. Grace gave her a kiss on the cheek. "Aunt Emily these are my best friends, Ella and Ava."

Aunt Emily hugged them both. "It is my pleasure to meet the two of you. We are going to have a fantastic day today. Wait until you see what I have prepared for you. David, will you load my baskets and the cooler into your vehicle for me?"

"Of course," he said and opened the trunk of her Mercedes. "Grace," he called out. "Can you hold this for a second?" He handed her a tray of what appeared to be appetizers. Then he grabbed the cooler and set it down on the ground before taking hold of the two picnic baskets. "Thanks." He closed the trunk and walked over to his Tahoe.

"Ella and Ava, come help us. Grab the rest," Grace said to them as Aunt Emily opened David's back hatch.

Aunt Emily had on a beautiful summer dress. Gold sandals and a matching hair pin. She smelled of Chanel. Grace knew the scent well. It was the exact same perfume Geraldine Prescott wore.

Ava smiled at Aunt Emily before saying, "I love your dress. Is that a Misa Los Angeles Hollen?"

"Yes," Aunt Emily replied. "Wow, you know a designer when you see one."

Ava smiled. "I love fabrics. Ella and I own a boutique. Textiles are my world."

"Do you have an online store?" Aunt Emily asked. "I would be happy to buy something from you."

"We do," Ava said and handed her their business card.

Aunt Emily smiled in return. "I love a smart business woman." She tucked the card in her pocket. "Are we ready?" She asked and everyone assured her they were eager to see what plans lie ahead.

"We have no idea where we are going," Grace told her as she got in the backseat.

David held the other passenger door open for Ella and Ava to get in, but Aunt Emily climbed in the backseat first so Ella sat up front with David.

"I want to hear more about your store," Aunt Emily said to Ava as she buckled her seatbelt.

Ava was delighted to oblige. She logged onto their website and showed Aunt Emily a few items from their fall lineup. "I designed this one myself."

"I love it!" Aunt Emily said and pointed to a pair of high waisted black dress pants. "I'll take five pairs of those. Lord knows I need them for my long trips to New York."

"Great," Ava said adding, "You're a size eight, right?"

"Very good," Aunt Emily replied.

When David drove over the Jamestown Bridge Ella asked, "Are we going to Newport?"

David gestured yes. "We'll be there in five minutes. I hope you all like boating."

Grace sat quietly looking out her window. Every now and then she saw David glance her way. She missed Hudson even more today. Seeing Ava and Ella brought back the memories of her life back home. *Home?* She thought. "I am nothing without you," she whispered.

Aunt Emily must have heard her because she tapped Grace on her knee and offered her a gentle smile.

Grace took a deep breath.

David pulled up to the dock and announced they had reached their destination. Standing there to greet them was his longtime friend and the captain of his vessel, William McGhee. Everyone got out and looked at all the gorgeous yachts, sailboats and boats.

"Ladies, this is Captain Bill." Bill kissed Aunt Emily on the cheek while his first mate unloaded David's vehicle.

"Aunt Emily, you look stunning as usual." Then he extended his hand to Grace. "You must be Grace."

"Yes," she replied and shook his hand before introducing him to Ava and Ella.

"Ella, Ava it is nice to meet the two of you. Come aboard." When he held his hand out, they both blew out a long breath.

"You're taking us out on the Bill Pay," Ella announced.

"Yes, I forgot you read the article on me in Hey Rhody Magazine."

Ella laughed at the thought of him knowing she saved every article ever written on him. She was fascinated about the person who turned a problem into a billion-dollar solution. "You intrigue me to say the least," she said to him.

"She's a beauty," Captain Bill said as he escorted the women aboard. "David would like for me to introduce you ladies to the Sunseeker while he and Aunt Emily prepare brunch." He held his hand out for Grace, Ella and Ava to follow him on the seventy-five-foot yacht.

"The wood is spectacular," Ava said as she ran her hand along the railing. "How do they get it so shiny?"

"They varnish the wood to protect it. You're looking at ten coats," Captain Bill said as he led the way to the living area.

"It is achingly beautiful," Ava said as she admired every detail.

Ella sat on the white leather sofa. "So is this." Then she got up and followed Captain Bill to the dining room and eventually to the galley where David had an array of beverages spread out on the counter for them. "Ooo, Mimosa," Ella said and handed Ava and Grace a glass. "Captain Bill?" She held a glass out to him, but he shook his head and told her not while he was on duty.

"The galley is fully stocked, wine cooler, ice maker, and to your right a wet bar. On the left is the sink and your appliances."

"Wow," Ava said as she opened the refrigerator. "Even the appliances are designed in the same wood."

"Up ahead is the helm with a very nice sitting area for you to bask in the sun, read or watch sailboats."

"And yachts," Ella said. "I have never seen so many gorgeous yachts in one place."

"I'll take you below before we go up to the top deck. There's also a bar, sitting area and an even nicer sun deck up there." He held his hand out for them to go down the spiral staircase.

"Look at the window design," Grace said peeking out the port hole before walking by the extended glass.

"This is the first salon suite complete with a separate shower and full-size bathroom. Every cabin has its own salon suite."

"Umm, how many bedrooms are there?" Grace asked.

"Four guests' quarters, the master cabin and below is the crew cabin also complete with its own ensuite, laundry room and storage space."

After touring the guest's quarters, they entered the master cabin.

"Wow. I know I keep saying that, but oh my goodness. How big is that TV?" Ava asked before sitting on the king-sized bed.

"Sixty-five inches," Captain Bill said as he opened the door to the bathroom.

"Of course, there are double sinks, a Jacuzzi and a huge shower," Ella said adding, "David deserves every ounce of this yacht."

Grace spun around almost bumping right into Ava. "Sorry," she announced and moved past her.

"You almost made me spill my drink," Ava announced and then proceeded to ask what was behind the next door.

"That is the secret stairway to the upper levels," Captain Bill said as he opened the door for them to go upstairs. As they were walking up, they heard the surround system come on. David was playing Keith Urban's "Somebody Like You."

"He plays a lot of Urban's songs," Captain Bill said and then asked them if they were ready to see the top deck. "I believe they are serving brunch on the flybridge."

"Where is the flybridge?" Ava asked.

"At the helm," Captain Bill said adding, "it has a very nice retractable sun roof."

When they reached the top deck Aunt Emily and David were waiting for them with what smelled amazingly delicious. Aunt Emily handed each of them a peach Bellini, before telling them she had fresh tropical fruit, raspberry baked French toast, a platter with homemade mini bagels, smoked salmon, flavored cream cheese with fresh dill and chopped scallions, capers, red onion slices, along with spinach quiche, and fluffy scrambled eggs. "Be sure to try Aunt Emily's whipped ricotta with honey on the mixed berries," David said as he handed everyone their plate.

"I'm starving," Ella said as she took her plate from his grip.

David teased her by holding onto the plate a little longer. "I'm kidding, here," he said as he let go.

Ella smirked letting him know she will get him later. "Payback," she told him as she walked up to help herself to the French toast.

Grace saw David give Captain Bill a thumbs up. "We're headed out to sea everyone," Captain Bill announced.

"That looks delicious," Aunt Emily said noticing the large shrimp, steamed clam and very large stalk of celery.

David pointed to Cory James, the first mate and said, "He makes the best bloody mary's."

"I'll take one please."

Cory James handed her the drink and told her, "No two are the same. It depends on what is in season."

Aunt Emily took her first sip, then another and drank half of the glass before telling him it was so good, she would like a second one. "Please."

Aunt Emily tapped David on the arm and nodded toward Grace. "How's she doing? Any word on the rascal who took her money?"

David inhaled before telling her he met with the detective. "Yeah, we caught him. You are never going to believe who it is," he said and sat down at the bar.

Aunt Emily followed his lead. They had their backs to the women. David looked over his shoulder and noticed Grace was talking to Ava and Ella while they were eating their brunch in the lounge area.

"Remember I had a bachelor party at my house a few weeks ago?"

"Yes," Aunt Emily said as she set her napkin down on the bar.

"Yeah, well one of the guests thought he could rent my house out without me finding out."

"Did you tell Grace?"

"No, I only found out yesterday. I knew her friends were coming and I wanted her to have a good time. I think she's comfortable at the beach house." He shook his head. "She doesn't even mind if I am around." David looked over his shoulder at Ella. "Her friends are nice. I'm glad they got to meet you, but I think Grace is keeping something from them. I expected them to be having ... I don't know more fun. Anyway, I have all her money."

"Who? For God's sake! Who on earth did this to the two of you?"

"One of Dale's friends, his name is George. The night of the party, he got up and said he needed to go to the bathroom, I thought he had food poisoning he was gone so long. The next day, he came back to the house and said he left his watch in the guest bathroom. I left him standing at the front door, but when I came back with his watch, he was standing in the kitchen right where I hang my keys. I didn't even notice he took the house key that night. He must have made a copy because when Grace showed me the key he left for her under my front mat, it was gold plated."

"That sneaky devil. Did you have him arrested?" She asked and got up.

"No, I'm waiting for Grace to decide."

"Never mind, you're in a bind with Dale right about now." Aunt Emily shook her head. "I'm going to get something to eat. Come on before everything gets cold."

David followed her to the display and helped himself to a sampling of everything. When Ella patted the seat next to where she was sitting David headed her way, but then she waved her finger at him.

"Not you, Aunt Emily, I'm kidding. Have a seat," she said smiling.

"Oh, Aunt Emily, everything was so good," Grace said as she got up and announced she was going for seconds. This was a day Grace would hold dear to her heart and remember for a long time to come.

Captain Bill was smooth. The women never even felt the yacht move until they looked up and saw open waters.

"Ladies," David said and held up his glass. "To the most beautiful group of women that have ever blessed the Bill Pay. I hope you enjoy your day and the fireworks even more. Cheers!"

"Cheers," everyone said in perfect unison.

"Fireworks?" Ava said. "From the yacht?"

"Is there a better place to see them?" Aunt Emily asked. "Just wait and see how spectacular they are from the harbor."

After an afternoon of dancing, sunbathing and laughing the ladies were ready to swim in the ocean. Aunt Emily was the first to dive in followed by Grace and Ella. David had to convince Ava there were no sharks nearby. "Don't worry Captain Bill has his ocean guardian device on."

"Okay, but how does the shark know that?" Ava asked still skeptical to go in the water.

"When a shark comes within a few meters of the shark shield, the strong electrical pulses emitted by the device cause the shark to experience safe but unbearable spasms in their receptors and they turn around and leave, just as humans do to a very bright light in the dark."

"Can I go in the hot tub instead?" She asked and David motioned for Cory James to assist her.

"Cory James, Ava would like to use the jacuzzi, can you please set the temperature to her comfort and liking?"

David could not help himself; he cannonballed right behind Ella causing her to spring up in the water.

Later the evening, they all sat together and watched the firework display. With every burst of color, Ava said, "Ahh."

When they returned home, Grace announced she was exhausted and went to her bedroom. Ava said she was going to her room to post all of her pictures on Instagram.

David asked Ella if she cared for a nightcap. Bourbon, wine or a beer. Ella knew David liked expensive bourbon so she asked for one.

They sat in the living room. "Oh my gosh!" She said. "I forgot how smooth good bourbon can taste."

"I'm glad you like it and I'm delighted Grace asked me to stay. I offered to go to the cabin, but she insisted I remain at the beach house."

"Yeah, Grace is unmoved by a lot of things. She's probably the strongest woman I know. I'm proud of her. She made a good life for herself." Ella snickered. "She makes good money. Saves every penny. In fact, I think she still has the first dollar she ever earned."

David got up and lit a fire. "I'm probably the only man who enjoys sitting fireside during the summer."

Ella caught sight of his eye's reflection from the glow. She sucked in a breath.

David sat down next to Ella on the sofa, took a sip and chuckled at the thought of Grace telling him she was calling the cops. "She can be feisty when she has to be--that's for sure. She stood her ground and hey," he held up his hands. "She let me stay." David smiled at Ella. "I'm glad I stayed. I got to meet you."

Ella tilted her head to the side not sure if he was being cordial or if he was being sincere and he was actually interested in her.

David leaned in and moved the hair from Ella's face. "You have brains, brawn and you are beautiful."

Ella looked into his eyes. "No one has ever said that to me."

"It's true," he said and poured them each another glass. "Do you like Harry Styles?"

"Yes," she said and took a swallow of her bourbon.

David got up and "One Direction-Night Changes" played on the stereo. Then he stoked the fire before asking if she wanted to take a stroll on the beach after they finished their cocktail.

Ella's heart was beating out of her chest. David had no idea how much she thought about him, read about him or longed to meet him. "Let's sit here a while longer. I'd like to enjoy this moment as long as I can."

He nodded and joined her on the couch, this time he sat right next to her. Caressing her hair with his fingers and telling her she was simply a breath of fresh air. "Being here with you is better than a walk on the beach."

"Oh, I wouldn't go that far," she teased. "I've seen a few sun rises and sets in my day. I'll bet yours are pretty spectacular."

David stood up, held his hand out for her. With his whiskey in one hand and the other around her waist, they danced to "How Deep Is Your Love" by the Bee Gees. When the song was over, Ella kissed David, but then apologized. "I'm sorry, I had too much to drink. I better go to my room, before—" She never put her glass down, she vanished in the dark.

David sat in the chair by the fireplace. Poured himself another bourbon and listened to Marvin Gaye sing, "What's Going On."

Chapter Twenty-Seven

E lla and Ava cried when they left David's house Sunday afternoon. "I'm going to miss you so much," Ella cried.

Grace wiped Ella's tears away and told her to come back anytime. Then she whispered in her ear, "I think David likes you."

Ella leaned back, shook her head and said, "I would never do that to you."

"What?" Grace put her hands on Ella's shoulders. "Trust me, I am not interested in him. Hudson is the love of my life. My heart will never get over losing him." She pursed her lips before saying, "Ella, David is a great guy, he's charming, kind and yes, he is the total package, but I don't look at him like that. I value him like a big brother. I'm grateful for both him and Aunt Emily right now and that is all there is. Please don't think otherwise."

"I'm worried about you. I want you to be happy. You are allowed to love more than one person."

Grace shook her head. "Not when you had a man like Hudson. My heart is going to need a lot of time to get over losing him. I'm still in love with him. I can feel his presence all around me."

They saw David carry Ava's bag out to the car. "Promise me, you will not worry or say a word about what we just talked about to anyone, especially Ava. I don't want her calling or texting me every five minutes telling me I have to move on."

They heard Ava telling David he was the best host she had ever met. "David, thank you so much for everything, for taking care of Grace, for allowing me to meet your aunt and my goodness for taking us out on your yacht. Best day of my life."

David hugged her and made her promise she would come back and visit. "My door is always open. I look forward to seeing you and Ella soon." He kissed her on the cheek and then put her bags in the trunk. "Ella, can I have a word with you."

Ella looked at Grace before replying, "Of course."

Grace carried the tote filled with snacks from Aunt Emily to the car. When she reached the backseat, she looked over her shoulder and saw David hugging Ella one last time. When Ella got in the driver's seat, she had tears in her eyes. Grace leaned in and squeezed her shoulder before saying, "I love you both. Call me when you get home and remember Aunt Emily will be visiting the boutique next week so take good care of her."

Ava leaned over and said, "Are you kidding me, I plan on giving her whatever she wants as long as I can take pictures of her in the store wearing my designs."

Ella backed out of the driveway as Ava waved goodbye to both David and Grace. Grace inhaled before turning around in time to see David blowing a kiss to them.

She walked up onto the front porch and asked if he would like to have a cup of tea with her.

"Sounds nice," he replied and shut the door. "I'll grab a scone for each of us."

"Grab me two please. One lemon, cranberry and one chocolate chip."

David took them to the living room and noticed he never turned the stereo off last night. He flipped the switch and sat down on the chair next to the fireplace. Grace came in holding two cups of green tea with coconut.

David took a sip and told her he liked Bangkok. "Harney and Sons have the best selections. Did you know their tea can be found around the world?"

Grace shook her head. "I didn't know that." First, she ate the lemon and cranberry scone, took a bite of the chocolate chip one and sipped her tea before saying, "David, I'm not sure where to start, but I would like to tell you about my visit to Point Judith."

David sat back holding his tea in both hands as he listened to Grace.

"Two weeks before my wedding, my fiancé passed away in what is known to be a tragic accident."

David set his tea down on the side table. "I am so sorry. Grace, is there anything, anything at all?"

She held up a hand, shook her head and explained, "He was supposed to have a simple procedure. An angiogram, but the lead surgeon allowed a trainee to perform the procedure and somehow, he ruptured the vein causing Hudson to die right there on the table. They tried telling me he had a heart attack, but we believe there is more to the story. His best friend hired an attorney." She held one finger up. "My heart aches for him, Melvin and Hudson have been friends all their lives."

"Grace, is there anything I can do?"

She gave him a wry smile. "You, have done so much already. I can never repay you for all that you have done for me, my friends and for my soul. Being here right now is exactly where I needed, to be" she sighed. "I'm surprised you didn't call the cops and tell them some crazy woman was in your home."

"You were far from crazy. Okay maybe a little." He took a deep breath before getting up and going over to the desk. "I demanded he give you cash." David put the money in Grace's hand. "I told him I wasn't sure if you planned on pressing charges, so for his sake he better do exactly what I said." David explained to Grace about the bachelor party and how he was able to get a key to David's house. "The fool actually thought he could get away with it. Can you imagine the surprise on his face when he discovered I never went to the cabin?"

Grace started to cry. Her tears turned to giggles before telling David that she was grateful.

"Grace, you can do whatever you want, but I'd like you to stay. I think you need more time to heal and hey what better place to be than at the ocean."

She nodded in agreement. "I swear you are the best male friend I have ever had the pleasure of knowing."

David yawned.

"David!" Grace swatted him and laughed. "That was a compliment."

He shook his head. "Sorry, we were up late last night. Ella and I were awake until three in the morning."

She lifted her head and smiled coquettishly. "Ella is an astonishing woman, she's the salt of the earth. I'm glad you had time to get to know her."

"I made her promise me; she would come back. I told her I was worried about you. I may have lied a little when I said she had to come back because she was the only person who could pull you out of this funk. In reality, I like her so I'm hoping she returns."

"For selfish reasons I am sure," Grace said. "Hmm, I think she likes you too. David, Hudson will always be the love of my life. I dream about him every night. Sometimes, during the day I can feel his presence. I don't know how to explain it, but in my heart, I knew he was with me the day I arrived in Point Judith and when I met you. Hudson gave me a sign; he made me feel good about being here."

"How long were the two of you together?"

She raised her eyebrows. "Four months and that is all it took for us to know we were meant for each other. He made me feel like I was the most important person in the world. I have never felt more loved than when I was with him." She smiled warmly adding, "He took my breath away with his love."

"Every person should know what that feels like," David said as he reached for the box of tissues. "Here," he said as her tears fell into her lap. "Grace, please stay. Aunt Emily and I like having you around."

"I'd like that," she replied. "Did Aunt Emily tell you she's going to Connecticut to visit Ava and Ella?"

"No, she didn't, but I know how impressed she was with them and their taste in clothing."

"David, I'm actually thinking of buying a home in Point Judith. Ava and Ella are busy with the boutique and we're only two hours away. I just feel like starting over. Back home I ran into so many people who expected to attend our wedding ... I just need to breathe a little while longer without worrying about explaining how I am doing, or holding up."

Chapter Twenty-Eight

A week later, David dropped Grace off at Aunt Emily's house so they could cook together and bond a little more. Aunt Emily told Grace she wanted to show her the house, her gardens and introduce her to Mediterranean cooking. David planned on spending the morning preparing his notes, going over his finances and getting his facts right on The Light House Inn project.

At ten o'clock sharp the bidding began. Geraldine kicked off the bid with one million dollars.

"Do I hear one point five?" the auctioneer announced.

David raised his hand and said, "Two million dollars."

"Two and a half," she called out.

David turned around and looked at her. It was the same woman he met at the town board meeting several months ago. Before David could counter someone else shouted.

"I'll give you three million." The man shouted over his laptop. Which meant he had a big shot somewhere in the world telling him how much money to bid.

David thought about the woman and wondered if she had the guy working for her. He noticed she didn't counter the three million, until David went to raise his sign.

"Three point five," she said, smiling like a Cheshire Cat.

That was five hundred thousand more than David wanted to pay for the property. Then as if on cue, the auctioneer announced there was a problem and they would have to continue the bidding next week. David looked at the clock and saw it was almost noon and had to wonder if the woman was in cahoots with the auctioneer. He stood up feeling deflated. Sick to his stomach. "Excuse me, but when will the bidding continue?"

Another woman stood up, grabbed her folder and said, "We will let everyone know by Monday."

David drove to Aunt Emily's house to pick Grace up. When he got there, he overheard them talking about going to see a doctor and he couldn't help wonder if his aunt was suggesting Grace see a therapist.

He shouted from the foyer. "Hello, where is everyone?"

"We're in the living room," Aunt Emily announced. "Come in and sit down." She stood up and poured him a cup of tea. "We are having your favorite. Peppermint tea with shortbread cookies dipped in chocolate."

David waved a hello to Grace as he sat on the sofa. "How was your day?" He asked as he accepted the tea cup and saucer.

"Thank you." He sat them both down on the side table waiting for Grace to respond, but she just looked at him.

"Are you okay?" She asked with concern on her face.

"David, what's wrong?" Aunt Emily asked and sat down next to him.

David kicked his legs out in front of him, ran his hands through his hair and blew out a long breath of air. "I may lose the inn."

Grace sat up. "Oh, no!"

Aunt Emily's hand went to her mouth. "To whom?"

David reached over, took a gulp of his tea, set the cup back down and said, "To the woman who wants to put a parking lot in."

"Oh, David, I am so sorry," Aunt Emily said and meant it. "What can I do?"

David sat up. "Can you find out if she has a cohort at the town hall?"

"What's her name?" Aunt Emily asked as she opened the drawer in the end table, took out a pen and piece of paper.

"Geraldine Prescott," he replied.

Grace jumped to her feet. "My Geraldine Prescott!"

"What?" David said.

"Thin woman about five-five with reddish brown hair."

"Yes," David said and he too stood up. "Do you know her?"

"Know her, she's my number one client. She buys large estates in need of repair and flips them for a handsome profit."

"Grace," Aunt Emily said. "Would you be willing to talk to her on David's behalf?"

Grace sat back down, pulled out her cellphone and showed Aunt Emily and David a picture of Miss Prescott before telling them more about her dealings with her.

"That's her," David said and sat back down.

"Miss Prescott has been buying property in New York, Connecticut, Massachusetts and Rhode Island for the past twenty years. She's worth a lot, but not as much as you David. Let me talk to her. Wait, what exactly does she want to do with the property?"

"Last I knew, she wants to put in a parking lot," he said.

Grace looked at her cellphone, punched a few numbers in and said, "Four million a year in revenue. I got this. David, we need to go home. Aunt Emily, I love you and I promise you I will let you know how we make out." Grace kissed her cheek and whispered in her ear. "It's my turn to help him."

When they got in the car, Grace was steady on her phone. "David, can you drive by the inn and let me take a look."

David drove slowly by The Lighthouse Inn. Grace got out of the car and took a few pictures before telling him an address to drive by. David pulled up and they both got out. It was about fifteen minutes away from the inn and it had a small building perfect for what Miss Prescott wanted to do with the property. "I'll call her when we get home." She looked at David before getting back in the car. "I don't want you to worry, I know what I am doing. If there is one thing I know, it's my clients and what makes them happy."

David was driving down Great Island Road until Grace shouted, "Stop, we need ice cream."

David pulled into The Sweet Shop and they both got out of the Tahoe. Grace ordered a double twist and David opted for a medium chocolate cone. They took their cones over to one of the big rocks along the parking lot and the water's edge, sat down and licked until their hearts were content. When Grace had enough, her stomach growled. "That was a lot. Phew, I can't take another lick. Let's go, we have an inn to save."

They both tossed their cones in the garbage, got back in the Tahoe and drove home in their own silence.

David parked the vehicle and said, "If you can't get her to change her mind, I won't hold it against you."

"David, David, David, you have so much to learn about me."

Grace opened the front door and was inside before he even opened his car door. Grace went in her room and logged on to her laptop. She sketched out a few details, wrote down some numbers and made a few calls before calling Miss Prescott.

"Grace? My dear, how are you?"

Grace rolled her eyes. "I am doing fine. Taking one day at time. How are you?" She asked even though she knew she was her amazing self.

"I'm good. When are you coming back to work? I miss you. In fact, I have been swimming solo," she said and Grace knew that meant she wasn't happy with whomever the office assigned her.

"I'm still in Rhode Island. Geraldine, I hear you are looking for a parcel of land."

Grace heard her clear her throat. "Yes, I am considering a purchase in Rhode Island."

"Geraldine, can you meet me tomorrow at––Grace gave her the address and told her to bring her wallet. I have something I know will interest you."

When Grace went out to find David, he was nowhere to be found. An hour later, he ran up the stairs from the beach. "Hey," he said with sweat pouring down his face.

"Are you okay?"

David nodded before heading to the kitchen. "It is what it is." He poured himself a glass of cold water, sat on the stool and shook his head several times. "I will never forgive myself if they tear down that inn and make it a parking lot."

Grace sat on the stool next to him. "Have faith. I'm meeting with Miss Prescott tomorrow morning. I believe I have the perfect solution. I found a shack on seven acres about twenty minutes outside of town and it's going for one point six million."

"Do you think she'll go for it?" he asked. "She was pretty adamant on buying the inn."

Grace tilted her head to the side and rolled her eyes at him. "Trust me, she is all about making a profit."

The following day Grace met with Geraldine Prescott. "Oh, sweetie, I am so sorry about your fiancé. What can I do to help you get through this difficult time?"

Grace gave her a hug and told her she would be fine. "All I need is a little time, love and support from my friends." Grace took two steps back. "You look amazing as usual."

"Darling, I appreciate you telling me that, but come on. You are hiding something. Out with it."

Grace held up one finger. "Give me a second." She felt like she was going to vomit. "I'm a little out of practice," she said and made her way toward her car. Grace took hold of her bottle of water and sipped it very slowly. "Ahh, okay." She carried the bottle back to where Miss Prescott was standing. "I hear you are looking for a new adventure in Rhode Island."

"Continue." Miss Prescott held her Vera Wang pocketbook in front of her, took a deep breath and waited for Grace to tell her what the meeting was all about. "You have my attention," she said.

Grace held her hands out in front of herself. "This would make the perfect parking lot. It even has a small building that could be used for a ticket booth." She waited for her to respond. "You don't even have to hire anyone; everything can be electronically."

"So, even when you are away until further notice you are still working. I see," Miss Prescott said unamused.

"Don't you want to know what the asking price is?" Grace opened the folder and handed a piece of paper to her as she explained, "The Lighthouse Inn is very special to my friend. Geraldine, I am asking you to consider this space as your parking lot. Here I ran the numbers." She handed her another document. "Over four million a year in revenue and it is close to both the ferry and the Jamestown Bridge."

"By any chance is your friend David Wayne?"

"He is," Grace replied. "Geraldine, he grew up right here in Point Judith the inn holds a special meaning for him. He has the funds to make the inn a family friendly place to stay."

"It might be too late. The deal is done. I was the highest bidder."

Grace was confused. "But they said the bidding would continue next week."

"Grace, the town doesn't want another failed hotel. It's settled."

"Not if *you*, withdraw your offer," Grace said a little louder than she had hoped to say. "I'm sorry," she said as she closed the folder.

"You've made me a lot of money in the past and I am grateful for it, but a deal is a deal. I have to go." Miss Prescott turned to leave, but then turned back around. "Mr. Wayne, has he helped you somehow?"

Grace stood frozen for a minute. With tears in her eyes she replied, "Tremendously."

Chapter Twenty-Nine

The planning board members were kind to David, at least two of them were. "Here," the older man said as he handed David a stack of files. "I suggest you start with all of the demolition applications."

David looked down noticing there were at least six or seven. He took a deep breath before assuring the gentleman he was up for the task. "I'll be fine," David said and asked if he could take the documents home with him.

The old guy shook his head. "You'll get it done quicker if you do it here. In case you have any questions," he added before walking away.

David made himself comfortable, opened the first manilla folder and read the instructions. The guy was right, in addition to the property address he needed the grid number.

"Here you go," a woman said putting a sticky note down next to a fresh cup of coffee. "Don't mind him, he likes to ruffle everyone's feathers." She winked. "They never make it easy. The identification number is the first thing they ask for, you would think they would hand it to you before all the paperwork. If you require anything else I'll be in my office."

"Thank you," David said. "Wait, what's your name?"

"Julie Kennedy," she replied.

"Thanks for the coffee."

David couldn't help himself. She was gorgeous. Auburn hair, big blue eyes and skin dripping in milk. "Hmm, she needs to be on the cover of Hey Rhody Magazine for being so kind, considerate, knowledgeable and beautiful." He chuckled to himself. "Town Hall's Finest!" He looked around the room knowing he had better get a move on before the clock sneaks to five and they kick him out. There were six demolition applications to be filled out. He started with the gas, then the electric, water, sewer, cable and phone company. It was his job to make sure they all disconnected the power supply from the street to the inn, then he had to submit everything in writing to the town.

David moved the pool application to the bottom of the pile. He worked on the application for the certificate letter from the asbestos testing agency and the engineer who would be submitting approval to the town, stating the location was free of any asbestos and or of its non-existence. Next up, was the copy of the demolition's contractor's certificate of liability insurance along with a check made out to the Town of Narragansett for fifty dollars to be returned when all debris was removed.

David started the application for the removal and relocation of the swimming pool and decided he would wait until he met with his architect, engineer and the surveyor to ensure he was within the town's setback requirements. Thankfully at his last meeting with the zoning board they instructed him to make sure he had two copies of the new swimming pool drawn to scale, including the setbacks, gates, fences and the required six-foot hedges to block any view from the neighboring business. The pool was his prize possession, he didn't want to mess it up or miss one detail. He looked up and saw it was already four o'clock. He wondered if Grace had taken anything out for dinner or if he should stop on his way home. Then he saw Julie walk out of her office.

"Do you need more time?" she asked.

"No, I'm all set," David replied, stood up and grabbed his paperwork. "I'll be back in a few days. I'm not in a rush as much as I want everything to be prefect."

Julie smiled. "I think what you are doing is wonderful. You're not just saving the inn; you're saving the town." She winked at him again and said, "Remember, when everything is complete the building inspector will come out one more time before issuing a statement declaring everything is done and in good standing. Once he gives you the letter with his seal on it, you'll be able to build your new inn."

"I can only hope," he said and followed her out the door.

When David reached his Tahoe, for the first time in a long time he thought about how nice it would be to have a woman in his life. As much as he wanted to call Ella and tell her how close he was to saving the inn, he didn't want to jinx himself and so he drove home.

Chapter Thirty

Grace met with Aunt Emily's gynecologist alone. She was scared something was wrong. Everything she read, all of her symptoms were pointing to her first thought, endometriosis. But when Dr. Cuveron walked in smiling, she took a sigh of relief thinking her periods were late because she was so stressed out.

"Grace, I have some good news. First, everything looks good." She sat down on the stool next to the bed and told Grace she wanted to do a sonogram. "Let's see how far along you are."

Grace snapped her chin forward.

"Yes, Grace you are pregnant." Dr. Cuveron performed the sonogram and determined Grace was twelve to thirteen weeks into her pregnancy. "I'm going to prescribe some prenatal vitamins for you." She took off her gloves and pushed her seat back to the metal table and said, "I'd like to see you start drinking a glass of orange juice every day." When she rolled herself back to where Grace was, she said, "I hope those are happy tears."

Grace held her hands over her face and nodded yes. "Thank you," she whispered and cried harder than ever before. Both Dr. Cuveron and her assistant rubbed Grace's arms and shoulders telling her the baby was in a good position and appeared to have a very healthy heart rate. Dr. Cuveron asked if she wanted to know the sex of the child. "I could do a blood test right now and tell you the baby's gender if you would like."

Grace blew her nose and said, "No, I want to be surprised. I don't care if it is a girl or a boy. I am just happy to be having our baby."

"Okay, if you're feeling okay, we'll leave you to get dressed. Unless there is someone you would like for us to call."

Grace gave the doctor a wry smile. "No, I'll be fine. Thank you so much."

When she reached her car, the temptation to call Ella and Ava was killing her. She wanted to share the news, but she had to do it in person. There was no way she wanted to miss seeing their face's when she told them. She already drove a wedge between them when she left for Rhode Island.

Grace drove straight to Aunt Emily's house. She felt guilty not calling Ella and Ava first, but Aunt Emily was the one who said she might be surprised by the results.

"Hello dear," Aunt Emily said into the phone.

"Hi, Aunt Emily by any chance are you home?"

"Yes, dear I am. Is everything okay? How did your appointment go?"

"I'm pulling into your driveway. I'll tell you when I come in," Grace said as she parked her car.

Aunt Emily met her at the front door. As soon as she saw Grace's glowing face she knew. Aunt Emily started clapping her hands. "Congratulations!" She hugged Grace and told her to come right in. "Oh Grace, I am so happy for you. You are going to make a wonderful mother. Hudson is surely smiling down upon you right now."

Grace's eyes started to fill up. She wiped them with the back of her hand and said, "God knew I needed him more than I ever did. Aunt Emily, I have never been happier in my life."

"How far along are you? Did she say?"

Grace took a deep breath and answered her. "About twelve weeks, but if my math is correct, I'm thinking more like thirteen."

"Come into the kitchen I have something for you." Aunt Emily gave her a bowl of hearty chickpea and spinach soup along with a stack of saltine crackers.

Grace sat down and declared it was her first meal of the day. "I was so nervous this morning, I couldn't eat." She took a bite, closed her eyes and moaned. When she opened her eyes she said, "This is heavenly."

Aunt Emily put a glass of lemon spritzer in front of Grace and watched her drink the entire glass before she could ask her if she would like some chocolate mousse. "You were famished. Would you care for some dessert? I have chocolate mousse along with a cranberry and walnut bread that goes wonderful-ly with my homemade lemon butter spread."

Grace sat back in her chair, looked at Aunt Emily and asked if she could take some home for David. "Can I take a little dessert home to give to David for when I tell him the news?"

"I have a complete dinner ready. I'll pack a basket right now. You go in the family room and put those feet up," Aunt Emily said as she pointed to the lounge chair in the corner near the bay window. "I'll be right back."

As soon as Aunt Emily gave Grace the basket she asked if she could go. "I can't wait to tell David the news."

"Go, and give him a hug from me. Grace, thank you ever so much for helping David. The inn is very special to him."

Grace smiled knowing just how much the inn meant to him. "I know it is and I'm so glad I was the one who helped him for a change."

When Grace got to the beach house David was not home. She set the basket on the counter and went into her room; she stood in front of the mirror with both hands on her belly and cried happy tears. Then she took the photo of Hudson into one of her hands, kissed it several times and told him, "We are having a baby." Her bottom lip quivered as she promised him, "I got this." Then she went over to the chase lounge and fell asleep until she heard David ask, "Did you go see Aunt Emily?"

Grace went out to the kitchen and hugged David.

"Hey, are you okay?" He asked.

"I'm great," she replied. "Aunt Emily made us dinner. Oh, and she made a chocolate mousse."

"Grace, what is going on? You…" He rubbed his chin. "Something is different about you."

She smiled before rubbing her belly. "David, I can't hold it in any longer. I'm pregnant."

David's eyes got wide. "Congratulations!" He put his arms around her and then quickly stood back. "How far along? Do you need me to do anything? Wow, you're having a baby. Okay. Hey, sit down."

"David, I'm having a baby. Women do it all the time. The baby won't be here until January." She sat on the kitchen stool at the counter and opened the basket looking for the chocolate mousse.

David helped her empty the basket and the two of them went out onto the back deck to celebrate.

Grace went to take her first bite; however, she pulled the spoon back out of her mouth. "How do you feel about me staying here until I find a house for me and the baby?"

David pointed his spoon at her. "You can stay here as long as you want. In fact, I want you to stay."

"Thank you," she replied and ate several bites. "I love my doctor. I want to be near her until the baby gets here and then I would like to start a new life for myself and the baby here in Point Judith." She inhaled before saying, "I know Hudson approves. I can feel it in my bones. Raising our son or daughter in this small fishing village is exactly where he would want us to be."

"I'm very happy for you. Can I get you anything?"

"A foot message would be nice." She chuckled. "I'm kidding."

David got up anyway. "I'll rub your feet." And with that he took hold of her foot and started with a deep message. When he was done, he asked her if she would like a cup of tea. "I see a lot of peppermint on the counter."

"It settles my stomach," she said and got up. After grabbing their dessert cups, she told him she wanted Aunt Emily's shortbread cookies. "This kid has a sweet tooth. I never craved sugar so much."

"Aunt Emily is going to be so excited for you." His face turned three shades of white. "We better make it clear..." he looked away.

"The baby is not yours," she said and took hold of two cookies filled with blueberry preserves. "She was the first person I consulted in."

The whistle on the tea kettle went off and David took hold of it as he jokingly said, "So I'm the last to know?"

Grace held her cup up. "No, I haven't told Ava and Ella yet. I want to tell them in person."

"Great, invite them for the weekend," he said as he filled her cup with hot water.

"Can we sit in the living room; my feet swell every afternoon and the only thing that seems to help is soaking them in the ocean or elevating them?"

"Grace the swimming pool at the cabin has salt water, we could move if you prefer."

"David, you are so sweet. God definitely put you on my path for a reason." Her eyes got big. "Do you think we could invite Ava and Ella to come and stay at the cabin during Columbus Day Weekend? I would like to have them here when I find out what the baby's gender is."

"Absolutely," he said and grabbed a cookie for himself.

"Hey, get your own," she teased.

"I have a great idea," he said. "We could use the cannon for the gender reveal."

"How?" She asked.

"I can fill it with either pink or blue smoke."

"I want to be surprised along with them. I'll ask my gynecologist to tell Aunt Emily and she can inform you."

"I'm glad you and Aunt Emily have become close," he said. "She admires and adores you very much."

"I was never close to my parents, so I really didn't know how to act when she offered to go with me to the doctor's. Then when I found out I was pregnant she was the first person I ran to see. She even told me she was delighted to be the baby's fairy godmother." Grace's eyes filled up. "Aunt Emily told me you are her greatest blessing in life and she couldn't be prouder of the man you have become." She wiped her eyes. "I want to be that kind of mother."

"You're both pretty special ladies."

Together they consumed all of the cookies but one. "I have got to go to the bathroom," Grace said contemplating if she wanted to grab the last cookie on her way. "They are going to be the reason I gain a hundred pounds this year."

David watched her leave and for a moment, he wished to be a dad. He picked up his cellphone, but then remembered Ella didn't know yet. Ella and David didn't talk much about their future dreams, marriage or children. They mostly talked about business and Grace. He wondered if she felt the chemistry between them because he did. Then again, there was that kiss.

"Ahh, much better," she said and sat back down.

David pushed the footstool in front of her. "Get used to it," he said smiling.

"Enough about my feet," she said. "Tell me about the inn and your thoughts on the overall design and I'll see if I can help."

David grabbed his clipboard along with some notes and his sketch showing where he hoped to put the swimming pool. "After touring the inn, I think I should take out the swimming pool and move it to another location. Maybe build a four-season room out back and house it there. I want to put in a new bar and combine two of the restaurants. I was thinking about a banquet room large enough to host meetings and large events."

"Like weddings?" She asked and leaned forward to take a better look.

"Yes," he said and handed her his sketch.

She looked it over for several minutes before saying, "What if you only served complimentary brunch and allowed your patrons to dine at all of the local restaurants?" She pursed her lips. "Point Judith has an amazing array of places to eat."

"You're absolutely right. The village has so many great restaurants, why take business from them."

"Maybe a few of the captains will host their daughter's weddings at the inn." She smiled. "After all, they are the reason you're doing all of this."

David sat back feeling good about everything. He knew Grace understood his reason for spending so much money on the old inn.

She slapped his knee. "Tell me more." She looked to the right. "Wait, I'm hungry. Let's feast on whatever else Aunt Emily's packed for us and work on your project while we eat."

"Grace, we should celebrate. I could not have done this without your help. I feel like taking you out for dinner. Let's go to the Spain Restaurant."

She smiled softly at him. "Thank you, but these feet are not going in any shoes right about now."

They warmed up the baked eggplant, tossed a salad and made peppermint iced tea. "Let's eat in the living room, you can put your feet up and use the TV tray," he said taking hold of their plates.

Grace grabbed the tea and followed him. She ate while listening to him tell her about ripping all of the sheetrock out and replacing it with shiplap. "I hate carpet, so I plan on putting down hardwood floors and ceramic tile."

"That's a big expense," she replied.

"Not as expensive as replacing all the copper pipes someone stole. I'm also going to replace all of the electric lines and I'm putting in a new security system. The building has good bones, but that is all that it has."

"I'm so proud of you." She glanced down and noticed he had two bridal––corporate suites in the design. "What are you including in the suites?"

"I stayed at a hotel in Greece that had a side room offering a nice lounge and bar area."

"Nice," she said. "Brides are going to love that. Women always have an entourage on their wedding day."

"And men love to hang out, smoke cigars, drink whiskey and talk about gorgeous women," he said smiling.

"Umm, did you make any ice cream this week?"

He laughed. "I did." He raised his eyebrows. "I made strawberry. Would you like a bowl?"

When she went to get up, he put his hand out like a stop sign. "Please, let me take care of you."

When he returned, he noticed Grace was reading his notes. He set her bowl down on the TV tray.

"Two hundred guest rooms, two suites, one restaurant, one banquet room, a bar, fire pit that seats fifty people, and the swimming pool." She looked up. "Filled with salt water, right?"

"Just for you," he replied and chuckled.

Grace put a spoonful of ice cream in her mouth, closed her eyes for second and said, "This is the best ice cream I have ever had."

David smiled from ear to ear. "I'm glad you like it."

"I'm going to get so fat living here." She finished her first bowl got up and asked if he wanted seconds.

He laughed. "No thanks."

When she returned, she asked what the four spaces were reserved for in front of the inn.

"Retail space."

Grace's eyes got wide.

David nodded knowing exactly what she was thinking. "I'm going to ask Ella if she wants to open a second shop here."

"Seriously?" She set her half-finished bowl of ice cream down on the end table.

"I'm prepared to offer them no rent for the first year."

Grace shook her head. "They will insist on paying you."

"Well, I won't take it. In fact, I plan on offering every one of my tenants free rent for the first year. Grace, the town has suffered enough. Seeing the inn crumble had to hurt local businesses. Point Judith needs a shot in the arm."

Grace thought about David and how generous he was when he saw Red at the dumpster. "You really are a good person. No wonder Ella admires you so much."

He smiled telling her, "I try to live my life not by my words, but how many lives I can make better."

Chapter
Thirty-One

B y the end of September, Grace was glowing. In spite of all her eating she had only gained eight pounds. Every time she looked at David, he shook his head as if to say I am not saying a word. "Don't look at me like that," he said to her. "Aunt Emily said I will find out when everyone else learns the sex of the baby."

Grace waved him off. "Hey, I was thinking about your idea for the inn to be family friendly and I was wondering if you considered putting in Murphy beds." She showed him a video of a twin and a double bed being pulled down from the wall. "What do you think?"

"I think it's a great idea. It saves me from storing extra roll away beds."

"Here, I did the math for the room along with a design showing you where they can be placed."

David looked at her drawing and saw she strategically positioned the beds so they would not interfere with the room's walking path. "One problem, where is the dresser?"

Grace winked. "Built into the wall." On her drawing, next to the clothing drawers was a coat closet that also contained an iron and a pull-down ironing board. "The television, refrigerator and microwave can be placed on shelves. Nowadays, smart TVs are slim enough to fit on a twelve-inch-deep shelf."

"See that's what I need, a woman's touch. Grace, I think your ideas are perfect!" Then he pointed to another set of knobs. "What are they for?"

"Ahh, fishing poles and a nice cooler on the bottom for the anglers to store their catch."

"So, when my guests walk in, they will see an open floor plan, a bed to sleep on and all the comforts of home." He kissed her on the cheek. "Thank you."

Grace leaned in and kissed him back. "You're welcome." She kissed him again, this time on his lips, but then quickly whispered, "I'm sorry. I don't know what came over me."

"Don't worry, we'll blame it on hormones."

Grace's face turned red. "That's it! I'm having a girl."

Then they heard a truck's back up beeper outside. David walked out the front door and called for Grace to come take a look. "Hey, it's a moving truck." David pointed to the right.

"Are they moving out?" She stepped outside watching two big box trucks park in their neighbor's driveway. The men started unloading several boxes and eventually furniture.

David said he was going to walk over and see what was going on. When he returned, he told Grace his neighbor sold the house to a doctor. "I didn't even know the house was for sale," he said and closed the door.

A week later, David and Grace met their new neighbor, Dr. Danny Ferris. A heart surgeon from Rhode Island Cardiology Center.

David put his hand out and introduced himself and Grace to Dr. Ferris. "Nice to meet you," David said. "Dr. Ferris this is my friend, Grace."

Dr. Ferris told them he was delighted to meet them and happy to see they were expecting a little one.

Grace smiled. "I'm having a baby. It's a long story, but David was kind enough to allow me to stay with him until the baby is born."

David tilted his head. "Welcome to the neighborhood."

They all laughed.

Dr. Ferris told them he was a single man getting ready to retire soon and always wanted to live at the beach. "I enjoy a good morning jog and an occasional swim in the ocean," he said. "How about the two of you?"

"I jog every morning before the sun comes up," David said.

Dr. Ferris pointed his finger at him. "So that was you the other morning. You know they make headbands with flashlights attached to them perfect for jogging or walking in the dark."

Grace caught the scent of ocean and deep-fried clams. "Would you like to join us for dinner?"

Dr. Ferris apologized and asked for a raincheck. "I'm on call this weekend. Perhaps we can all get together in the near future."

"Sounds good," David said.

"Have a good weekend," Grace told him and then followed David back to the house.

"He seems nice," David said as he opened the front door for Grace.

"I smell food," she said laughingly.

"Someone's hungry," he said. "Would you like to order take out?"

"Yes," she said and asked if they could get chowder and fried clams from Champlin's Seafood.

"Grace, if you think your feet are swollen now, wait until you eat fried food. Are you sure?"

"Hey, I thought the doctor lived next door? You're right. But if we share an order of fried clams," she laughingly added, "it will be half the calories. Besides, my doctor said I was doing great with my weight gain and your little admirer is craving fried clams."

He laughed. "Anything for the baby!" Then he called their order in and told her it would be delivered in twenty minutes. "I'll set the table out on the back deck. What would you like to drink?"

"Water with lemon, please."

David saw something in her that day. She was relaxed, comfortable and she began joking with people and that was a good sign.

Chapter Thirty-Two

Geraldine Prescott decided not to invest in the Rhode Island parking lot, instead she purchased a home for herself on Watch Hill. Grace was delighted to show her the property and to introduce her to Aunt Emily. The two women hit it off the moment they knew they had a few things in common--they both loved being single, running their own empires and drinking Diamonds Are Forever Martinis. The cocktail was too fancy and expensive for Grace's taste. It's made with chilled Absolute Elyx vodka, a hint of fresh lime juice, stirred or shaken, and it had a sparkling one carat diamond at the bottom of the glass. When Grace asked where on earth they drank the cocktail, in perfect unison Aunt Emily and Miss Prescott responded, "The Ritz-Carlton in Tokyo."

When Grace got home and told David about Miss Prescott's and Aunt Emily's taste for expensive cocktails, he told her she made a match in heaven. "I'm delighted Aunt Emily has a new friend she can travel around the world with, dine at the finer restaurants and share fancy drinks with, because I would never pay that kind of money for one damn cocktail."

Grace thought about what David had said. He was a lot like Ella, frugal about money and not willing to spend it on extravagant items. "Are you excited about tomorrow?" She asked knowing he was about to explode seeing his dream come to life.

"I feel like I am about to give birth. A part of me would have died seeing them tear down that inn. I had to save it."

"I agree," she said and then told him she was taking him out to dinner. "I made reservations for us at the Spain Restaurant for seven."

"Seriously," he said.

"Yes, now get dressed." She was wearing a summer dress and based on the photos taken at the restaurant she was dressed appropriately and ready to walk out the door. The only thing she did grab was her wallet and a lace shawl.

David and Grace celebrated his new adventure. "I could not have done this without you," he said and held up his Ginger Ale. "Cheers to the baby and to the new Lighthouse Inn."

"Cheers," Grace said and sipped her water.

Monday morning, David sat in his lawyer's office knowing he was about to accomplish something wonderful. The town accepted his bid, the board of health was satisfied with his demolition and renovation plans.

"Are you ready to sign your life away?" David's attorney asked as he handed him the final document. "You're doing a good deed rebuilding the old Dutch Inn."

David smiled remembering the many days swimming in the pool with Allan by his side. "We sure do have some great memories in the old establishment."

"Have you decided on a name yet," Allan asked as he handed David a folder.

"The Lighthouse Inn of Galilee," David replied. "I'm going to keep the name as is. I'm hoping people come back and support our local businesses."

"You always did have a passion for lighthouses."

After all the documents were signed his attorney handed him a Cuban cigar. Then he proceeded to light it for him before lighting his own. "Did I see a line of dumpsters and dump trucks on the property this morning?"

"You sure did," David replied and stood up. "Thanks for the cigar and for being here. I appreciate you scheduling it so fast." David's lawyer was sharp as a tack when it came to real estate closings, he knew how to get them closed in no time.

David drove from Newport to Point Judith in less than twenty minutes. He was so excited to get started. The first task at hand was taking out all of the asbestos and black mold. His lead contractor hired a fully licensed and insured company coupled with the experience and knowledge to get the job done in a third of the time. When David saw all the white plastic stretching from one end of the inn to the other, he knew those guys took removal seriously. Signs were everywhere. "No Admittance" David met the lead contractor at the gate. "How was your closing this morning?" John asked.

"Good, we're all set."

John motioned for his crew chief to get things started. "I have everything in place. The box trucks are ready to take away the contaminated material, the dump trucks are lined up and ready to haul away the pool material and the dumpsters are for everything else."

While no one was allowed inside until the inspector signed off on the removal of all asbestos, they were allowed to start on the old swimming pool. The entire area was secured using heavy plastic, clear tape and caution tape. Sixteen men all dressed in white overalls and gas masks walked by David giving John a thumbs up. By the time John was done with the structure the only thing left standing would be the steel frame.

David was impressed with the organization of the project. Every dumpster had a label. Tile, wood, glass, furniture, paper, etcetera. "I don't see a spot for all of the metal tables?"

John pointed to a flatbed truck. "As soon as I can get in the kitchen, we're taking it to the recycling facility for cleaning and then off to your new location."

"Sounds like you have it all under control," David said. "What can I do to make things go smooth?"

John laughed aloud. "Just be ready to spend some money." John patted David on the back. "Your bookkeeper has everything under control."

David went to say goodbye, but then asked, "How did you get the hazmat team in there before the closing?"

"Huh, my wife Renee works for the board of health. She may have put the wrong start date on the form. If we're done here, I have work to do."

David could not wait to get things started. He wanted to see the building come to life. Not being able to go inside he decided to go home and share his news with Grace. When he got home, he saw a note on the cork board. "Gone house hunting. See you for dinner out on the back deck!"

His heart wasn't sure how to feel about her moving out. He certainly was not in love with her, but he did enjoy having her around. They made a good team. She was a tremendous help to him and the inn.

An hour later, Grace walked in with a pizza from On Point Pizza. "I hope you like pepperoni," she said and put her bag on the floor.

David held his hand out and put the pizza on the warming tray. "I do," he replied.

"So, I have some good news. I put a bid on a small house today."

"Seriously?" He said as he took hold of two plates.

"Yeah, but it needs some work so I won't be able to move in until after the baby is born."

"Whereabouts?" He handed her a plate.

"Succotash Road in South Kingston, it's perfect. It has views of Potter Pond and it's only fifteen minutes away." Grace put two slices of pizza on her plate and helped herself to a glass of iced tea.

David took hold of his plate and sat down next to her. "I'm delighted you decided to stay in Point Judith."

She smiled and said, "Aunt Emily said the exact same thing to me today." Then she took a bite of her pizza and winked.

Chapter Thirty-Three

Grace was so excited to see Ella and Ava, she could hardly contain herself. She stood in front of the mirror, putting on one sweater after another, finally putting on the new navy-blue sweatshirt bearing a large red lobster on the front. "Perfect! Ava will think the idea was hers." She stood sideways one more time before going out to the kitchen. "David?" she called out. Then she went out onto the back deck. "Huh?"

"There you are," he said putting his hand on her shoulder. "Don't turn around. I have a surprise for you." He set the seat on the floor and told her, "Okay now you can look."

Grace spun around and saw an Orbit baby stroller and ride travel system in black and rose gold. Her hands went to her mouth as tears fell from her eyes.

David gave her a hug. "I wanted to be the first person to buy the baby something. It goes great in the sand and you can bring the little one home from the hospital in it."

Grace held out her hand. David laced his fingers in hers. "Thank you so much. I love it and so will the baby."

"I'll hide it up in my office until we come back from the cabin," he said and rolled it inside. "Come on, or we'll be late."

"Right, they're meeting us at the cabin. Did you call Aunt Emily?" Grace asked as she closed the back door, but then noticed a large white feather had dropped on the round patio table. Grace opened the door and went back outside to pick it up, but the wind carried it away. She stood there watching as it drifted toward the new neighbor's house. She looked up knowing Hudson was with her. "At least you know what we are having," she whispered and went back inside.

David came down from his office singing, "Good Times" by Sam Cooke. "The clock on the wall says it's time to go."

Grace shook her head and smiled as she followed him out the front door. As soon as she got in the vehicle her stomach rumbled in anticipation, she could feel her body flush all the way down to her toes. She smiled and sent a chef's kiss to the sky. The sun overhead was high and in a split second two things happened: first she gasped, then with every ounce of her body she smiled, her dream of becoming a mother will soon be her reality.

David was driving on Galilee Escape Road when an MG convertible pulled up alongside of him with the radio blaring and two gorgeous women singing at the top of their lungs. David never once turned his head to look at them. Grace admired that about him, he was respectful of her presence. After all, how were the two women flirting with him to know if he was her man or not. She could only hope Ella took David up on his offer, moved to Point Judith and fell in love with him. Ella deserved to be loved by someone special and so does David. She looked over at him. *Hudson would have liked you.*

When they arrived at the cabin, Aunt Emily was standing on the front porch waving. Grace turned to David. "I'm officially adopting her as my fairy godmother."

David waved back to Aunt Emily and told Grace there was no way Aunt Emily was going to miss this day or prepare a feast. "She loves you. I can see it and hear it in her voice every time she asks me how you are holding up."

At that moment, Grace understood the meaning of family and friends. "I am holding up just fine," she said. When she got out of the Tahoe, her knees were shaking, she thought she was going to collapse. "I can't believe how nervous I am," she said and held onto the door handle. "This is it. I learn the sex of our baby." She looked up. "Stay with me."

David walked around to where she was, first he gently touched her arm, but as soon as they made eye contact, he held her close in his arms as they made their way up the steps.

Aunt Emily noticed Grace was a bit pale. "Come with me," she said. "I have something to perk you up." She handed her a crisp Golden Delicious apple. "I'll make you a cup of tea. What time are your friends expected?"

"Eleven o'clock," Grace replied and sat down in the over-sized chair in front of the bay window.

David looked up at the clock. "We have an hour before they arrive," he said and proceeded to help Aunt Emily in the kitchen.

Grace could hear them talking about keeping her off her feet today. "Keep a close eye on her," Aunt Emily said as she set the tea pot, cup and saucer filled with saltine crackers down. By the time she reached Grace she had eaten the entire apple. "Good for you," she said as she handed Grace her tea. "Do you feel better?"

"I do," Grace replied as she reached for a cracker. "This baby is always hungry."

"Well, you look great," David said standing behind them. "Would anyone care for me to light a fire?" The temperature was supposed to be in the low seventies. David had planned on sitting around the fire pit immediately after the reveal, but now he's thinking with Grace not feeling so well, perhaps they should all sit inside? "Would you like to spend the afternoon outdoors or inside," he asked standing in front of Grace holding several logs in his hands.

"Outside," she replied and then told him she felt much better. When she stood up both Aunt Emily and David reached for her. Grace laughed. "What am I going to do with the two of you? I am only going to the bathroom. Trust me, I am okay."

Once inside she let out a huge pocket of gas. "Ahh." She sat
down and peed for what seemed an hour. When she returned
to the family room, she noticed Aunt Emily and David waving
to Ella and Ava's car. Grace stepped out onto the front porch
and said on a tail end of a sob, "My heart is going to explode
today."

Silence followed. Neither David or Aunt Emily wanted to
take one moment of Grace's joy from her. It was her special day
and she was allowed to feel any way she desired. Ava hugged her
first and when Ella reached for her, Grace tenderly hugged her
tighter. Grace needed her friends––all of them, Aunt Emily,
David, Ava and especially Ella. Tears ran down her face. The
thought of having a baby and Hudson not being with her
suddenly crippled her mentally. Her emotions were all over the
place. Grace looked up at the sky, wiped away her tears, trying
to make sense of her life. Ella leaned in and rested her head on
Grace's shoulder. Grace kept her eyes closed until Ella stood
back to give her a pep talk. "Stop crying, we missed you too,
but damn girl, everything about this summer looks good on
you."

When Grace and Aunt Emily made eye contact, Grace
winked.

"Come on, let's go," Aunt Emily said aloud and everyone
followed her inside. "I have lunch ready in the kitchen. Help
yourself and take a seat in the living room. David did you light
the fire yet?"

David laughed. "I thought we were going outside?" He replied before saying, "Yes, Ma'am."

"Grace, remember the day we skipped school?" Ava said as she filled her plate with a tomato crostini and a big juicy burger topped with spinach, tomato and blue cheese.

"Yes," Grace said as she too filled her plate with one of every-thing on the counter. "That was the most perfect summer day. We went to the lighthouse in?"

"The Stratford Point Lighthouse," Ella said as she walked toward the living room hoping to get a seat next to the fire place.

Ava followed her into the living room and sat beside her. "I was so happy that day. We were together and no one was there to bother us or tell us what to do. Every day should be as lazy," she said and took a bite of her burger.

"That was the happiest day of my senior year," Ella said. "We were young, free spirits, tan and we were all excited about our futures. Grace wanted to work in real estate and I wanted to own my own business."

"Hey, me too," Ava said as she dropped her napkin on the floor.

"Yeah, we were full of zealous and dreams," Ella said.

Aunt Emily sat on the other end of the couch. When she pointed toward the recliner Grace took her advice, sat down and lifted her feet up.

"It sounds like all of your dreams came true," Aunt Emily announced, smiling at Ava.

David smiled back at Ella as he sat to her left. "I got your text the other day. You were right about setting up an emergency fund. Thanks."

Grace smiled knowing they both thought alike. Had heads for business and knew how to make buck or two. She offered a Saccharine sweet smile when her eyes met David's. Enough about them, she had to know. She pushed her plate away and sat up. She was dying inside. As soon as everyone finished eating Grace was ready for the reveal. She looked at David and raised her eyebrows, but he continued listening to Ella as she spoke about expanding one of their clothing lines. "We want to add a new men's sport line to our store. What do you think?"

He let her words soak in before raising an arched brow. "Sounds great," he replied and stood up. "Grace, what do you say we take this party outside. Are you ready?"

Ella's eyes shot over toward Grace. She thought she was all for her and David getting together, but it doesn't feel that way now.

David knocked his knuckles on the table. "Come on." He moved closer to her and whispered, "You got this."

Grace put her feet down and told Ella and Ava she had a surprise for them waiting outside.

Ella snorted as if amused. "Another expensive handbag?"

Silence hung over them as Grace mulled over her words. "No, much bigger," she replied.

Everyone set his and her dishes in the kitchen sink. Grabbed a glass of apple cider and followed David outside. There was table and chairs set up next to the fire pit along with two small boxes. Grace took hold of the boxes and handed them to Ava and Ella.

Grace swallowed the lump in her throat, cupped her chin before saying, "I will always treasure the time I spent with Hudson and I know he would want the two of you to be a part of our lives." Grace forced a smile at David. "I'm fine," she said and took a long sip of her cider.

Aunt Emily's hand was resting on David's shoulder. "She'll be fine," she whispered.

David moved a chair her way, but Grace just smiled at him as she continued. "I wanted to wait until the two of you could be here with Aunt Emily, David and myself." Grace felt a wave of excitement come over her.

Ella looked at David and then at Grace. Then she glanced down at Grace's left hand.

"Are you okay?" Ava asked.

Grace smiled from ear to ear. Aunt Emily bowed her head and David moved closer toward the cannon. First Grace sat down and then she asked Ava and Ella to open their gifts. "You might want to sit down before you open your gifts," she said.

Aunt Emily took Ava by the hand and sat her down on Grace's right, then she told Ella to sit on the other side of Grace. When Ava opened her box first, Aunt Emily told her to breathe. Ella could not hold back her tears. She was gushing. Inside they both found a lighthouse and a sweatshirt with the word "Auntie" in front of their names. The notecard asked them to be baby Harbor's godmother.

Grace unable to speak. Whispered brokenly, "I'm having a baby."

They both got up and hugged her.

Aunt Emily stood back with tears in her eyes. She genuinely loved Grace and she was happy for her. David put his arm around his aunt and kissed her temple.

Grace peeked her face through and asked if they wanted to know the sex of the baby. "I didn't want to know the sex of the baby until the two of you could be here."

"How?" Ava asked.

"Ava," Ella said.

"No seriously, it's okay," Grace said. "I'm five months pregnant."

Ava clapped her hands. "I'm going to make all of her clothes." She put her hands to her mouth. "His too, if it's a boy," she laughingly added.

David approached Grace and asked if she was ready for the baby reveal. "Are you ready to fire off the cannon?"

Grace held out her hand as David helped her up. "This Momma is more than ready."

As Grace, Aunt Emily, Ella and Ava stood back and watched David ignite the gunpowder by means of a timed fuse their tears of joy flowed. David stepped to the side as blue smoke filled the air.

Chapter Thirty-Four

David wasted no time. As soon as he got word there was a snag at the inn, he headed over to the construction site. He had a plan for everything. The entire project was mapped out according to his timeline and if everything went smoothly, the inn would be ready to open in two years. He hired the best foreman around to oversee the project. John understood David's desire to get the inn open as soon as possible. When he pulled up to the site, he was met by two burly men and a young fellow. David extended his hand to them. Thankfully, his foreman made sure every man wore either a tee shirt, sweatshirt or jacket bearing each of their names. He didn't want any trouble from the board of health, Workers' comp or from OSHA. Only those working on the project were supposed to be on the property. "Thank you so much for signing on," David told them.

"We actually wanted to thank you. Until this project came along, none of us were working." The men held their hands out to shake David's hand.

"David," John said standing behind him. "Hey, listen we ran into a problem."

The men waved goodbye and went on about their work, leaving John to tell David about the setback.

"I'll see you guys later," John called out to them and David echoed his sentiments.

"It looks like the old oil tank suffered some damage and a little deterioration and that means you have contaminated soil. You're going to have to call in a company that can remove the tank and the dirt."

David ran his hands through is hair. "Hold on. I thought the tank was in the building."

"Yeah, no," John replied. "That's the original tank. The owner of the Dutch Inn put that in years ago. It's been empty for decades. The new owner replaced it with a thousand-gallon tank back in 1998 when he renovated the place. Whoever put it in didn't bury it deep enough. That was mistake number one. The other problem is they put it in too close to the septic line and I think," John raised his hands, palms up. "They damaged the side of the tank." John shook his head. "All I can tell you is it's not going to be a cheap fix."

"I don't care about the money," David said. "I want it done right. Do you know someone who can take care of it?"

John handed David a business card.

David read the name, "Vaz-Co, okay, I'll call them now." He pulled out his cellphone and pointed to the men walking away. He was glad John hired them. They seemed to appreciate the work. "They seem like really great guys."

"They are," John said as he started to follow them.

"Wait, how's everything else going?" David asked.

"Great," John said. "The mini excavator and skid steer were delivered an hour ago. We just started jackhammering the cement. As fast as we get it loose with the demolition saw, we take it outside and load it in the tri-axle."

"All right, let me call this guy and see how soon he can get someone over here to remove the oil tank." David looked at the card and saw it was a woman's name. He dialed the number and sure enough a female answered the phone. "Vaz-Co reclaiming services, how can I help you?"

"Christina?"

"Yes."

"Hi, my name is David Wayne and one of my contractors discovered a hole in a buried oil tank."

"Okay, what's the location? I'll send someone out there right away."

David gave her the address and within an hour an elderly gentleman was there to let him know it would cost him seventy-five thousand dollars to have the tank and the soil removed.

"When can you do it?" David asked.

"Tomorrow," Ibrahim replied.

"Thank you, do you need a deposit?"

"No, no," he replied. "I will give you a bill when the job is complete. Let me call Christina and tell her to send the crew here first thing in the morning."

After they shook hands, David went inside to see how far along the men were with removal of the old pool. "Wow," he said, but no one heard him amongst the noise. Then he went upstairs to check on the guest's rooms located at the back of the inn. He was surprised to see most of the sheetrock was gone. Below were three large dumpsters filled with sheetrock, carpeting and tile. He almost bumped into one of the men as the man carried an armload of sheetrock out of one of a room. "Excuse me," the man said to David. "Sorry, but you're not supposed to be up here." Then he dropped his load into the waiting dumpster below.

David raised his hand as if to say I'm out of here and apologized for getting in his way. "You're right. I'm leaving." Then he laughed to himself. "I better get myself a name tag."

Six months later, the only thing left standing was the building's frame. On the North side of the building stacked under large pieces of plastic was the new building material, to the right a makeshift tent for cutting tile and to the left of that were spools of wire. They were ready for the construction to begin. The new pool had been excavated, the foundation secured and approved by the engineer, architect and the town. As soon as the new roof was finished, John started on the exterior framing, masonry work, and the siding. Almost a year later, David was excited to see the interior start to come to life. "How long do you think it will take to complete all of the interior rooms?" David asked.

John laughed, "I was waiting for you to ask. Relax, a year from now you can open your inn."

David nodded.

John patted David on the back. "We're right on schedule."

Chapter Thirty-Five

Ella wanted the shop to have the same exact floor plan as the boutique in Connecticut, but Ava wanted something entirely different. She insisted her new clothing lines stand out front and center. "We don't have the same amount of floor space," Ava declared and she was right. The Beach Boutique had three thousand square feet, in Point Judith there was half.

"Fine, design it the way you want," Ella said and walked into her office. She looked at her cell phone for the tenth time that morning. Nothing, not even a reply message back from David. In less than three months she would have to make a decision. Stay in Connecticut or move to Rhode Island and be with her best friends. The Beach Boutique was well established, known for offering the finest beachwear along the Connecticut shoreline; it no longer required Ella or Ava be on location twenty-four-seven. Olivia was known by everyone as the friendliest sales person around. Men and women adored her for her attention to detail and friendly service. Ella sat at her desk pondering the thought of leaving her first baby in the hands of Olivia and...the frightful thought of seeing David and Grace together.

"Hey," Ava said as she tapped on Ella's door. "Can I come in?"

"Of course, you can," Ella said and turned her phone over. "What's up?"

"Are you mad at me?"

"No, why do you ask?"

"You seem upset."

As much as Ella felt sick for even considering spending time with David knowing he clearly enjoyed being with Grace. She couldn't lie to Ava. For some reason Ava always knew. She sipped her coffee as if pondering her thoughts on whether or not she should open up to her. This was not a decision she knew she needed to make at the moment. Still, Ava deserved to know.

A brief smile came and went from Ava's face.

"I'm not sure I want to move to Rhode Island."

A look of shock replaces Ava's smile. "What? Why not? I thought we were doing this together. You said you trusted Olivia to run the place." Ava moved closer to get a better look at Ella. "Look at me. You're not telling me something. Don't lie to me." She waved her finger at Ella. "You know I can tell and besides, I."

"What?" Ella stood up. "You what?"

"Phillip loves the idea of me moving to Rhode Island and I think he's going to ask me to marry him."

Ella collapsed back in her chair. Silence hung over them as Ella mulled over Ava's words.

Ava kept her mouth closed. Then it sagged before she opened it. "I have never felt this way about a man before."

Ella rubbed her head. "You said that about Jimmy, remember?"

"This is different." She held her hands as if in prayer. "He's taking me away this weekend. I seriously think he's going to propose."

Ella shook her head. "Why do you think that?"

"Because, he told me to make sure I get my nails done and bring my cell phone. Apparently, I forgot it one day and he wanted me to take a picture of us at a fancy restaurant in New York."

Ella raised her hand for Ava to stop continuing any further. "Please tell me he is not the guy who sent you flowers."

Ava cracked a smile.

"Ava! Seriously, how long before you decide he's not the one for you?" As soon as Ella said the words, she regretted saying them. "I'm sorry. I worry about you. I just don't want you to make a mistake that you will regret for the rest of your life."

"I love Phillip. Honestly, I do."

"Give me a hug you big pile of lust."

They embraced right before they heard the bell on the front door and they knew a customer had arrived. Ella glanced over at the security system and saw three women heading for the hat rack. "We have customers. We'll talk about this later. I promise," she told Ava and followed her to the front of the store.

Fall turned to winter and before they knew it, they were ordering and sending merchandise to the new location.

"Are you excited about this weekend?" Ava asked. "We get to see Hudson."

"I am excited to see him. I hope he likes his birthday present."

"He will. What little boy wouldn't want a new bike?" Ava said. "I bought two helmets just in case one is too big for his little head."

Ella rubbed her chin. "Do you think we should have gotten him one of those cool Jeeps to drive on the beach instead of a tricycle?"

Ava waved her hand in the air. "No, let his mother buy the expensive stuff." She laughed. "She makes more money than we do. Besides he's only two."

Ella shook her head. "Sit down." Then she pulled out a spreadsheet and handed it to Ava.

Ava read the number at the bottom three times. "We?" And by the way her voice dipped Ella knew she read it correctly.

Ava held the paper to her chest and started to cry.

"We did it!" Ella said in a calm and confident voice. "We made our first million dollars."

"How?" Ava asked surprised she hadn't noticed.

"We have been averaging about twenty-seven hundred a day. I didn't realize it either until I met with the accountant. We've been so busy with customers, designing the new clothing lines and planning the new location, I hadn't had the time to sit down and run the numbers."

"This calls for a celebration," Ava said and hugged Ella. "Let's go out for dinner."

Ella knew she was meeting Philip. "It's okay, go."

Friday morning, Ella and Ava told Olivia to call if she had any questions. "If you have any concerns whatsoever call me," Ella said.

Ella made sure she hired extra staff for the weekend so Olivia wouldn't feel overwhelmed. When they got in the car Ava told her she was sending in a spy to make sure the place was being run efficiently.

Ella laughed so loud Ava jumped. "Olivia will kick your ass if she finds out."

Ella and Ava made it to Point Judith in less than two hours. When they arrived at the new store boxes were stacked up as high as the ceiling. Thankfully Aunt Emily sent over her crew to help unbox and put merchandise on the shelves and dresses on hangers. "My goodness," Ava shouted. "Everything needs to be steam ironed."

"Relax," one woman told her. "It's olefin. It's naturally resistant to wrinkles. One hour and you'll never know it came out of a box."

"Huh," Ella said to Ava.

"Hello!" Grace announced as Hudson ran ahead of her.

Ava picked him up and kissed his face before Ella took hold of him and said, "Wait until you see what we bought you for your birthday."

"I'm going to be two," Hudson said.

"Yes, you are and Aunt Ella loves you two times more."

When Hudson kissed her cheek, her heart melted. She looked at Grace and thought how lucky and blessed she was. She set Hudson down and told him there was a new slide in the play area. "Hey," Ella said as she hugged Grace.

"What can I do?" Grace asked but then raised her hand in the air. "I know hang the pants up." Then she handed Hudson his tote bag, his sippy cup and told him to go over to the play area and behave himself. As small as the space was Ava and Ella made room for Hudson by putting in a five-by-five-foot enclosed area filled with all of his favorite toys, games and books.

At four o'clock on Sunday the store was ready to greet its first customer. "My back is killing me," Ava announced.

"Please, my back never stopped hurting when I was carrying Hudson. I had to take one Advil and one Tylenol to make the pain go away."

Ella turned to face Ava.

"Not on your life," Ava said to her. "I make him wear a rubber and I still get the shot every month. Besides, we'd have to have sex in order for me to even get pregnant."

"Hello," Aunt Emily called out.

Grace smiled at Ava and Ella. "Aunt Emily wanted to bring you a gift basket."

"Food I hope," Ella said as she made her way to greet Aunt Emily. "You are the best!" Ella only had to inhale once to know her favorite summer skillet with clams, sausage and corn was in the basket.

"The store looks amazing!" Aunt Emily said as she handed the basket to Ella.

Ella gave her a kiss on both cheeks before telling her, "Wait until you see the clothing line Ava designed just for you."

Ava put her hand on the small of Aunt Emily's back. "You can ride for hours wearing my designs and no one will ever know you stepped out of a car."

"Hello, sweetheart." Aunt Emily kissed Ava and told her the store was exactly what she had hoped it would be. "Gorgeous!" Then she pointed to the play area. "I see my favorite godson?" She walked over to pick him up, but he was sleeping on his baby whale cuddle pillow. She kissed his forehead and moved the blue and white sailboat to the side.

"The store looks great," David said.

Aunt Emily held her finger to her lips. "Shhhh, Hudson is sound asleep."

"Sorry," he whispered. Then he waved to Ella. "Hey, can I see you for a minute?"

Now, he wants to see me. I've been here for three days and now he has time for me. "Sure, I'm dying to take a break. Let's go outside," she said giving him an impish grin. "I could use some fresh air."

David went to kiss her on the cheek, but she turned and looked the other way. "Are you okay?"

"I'm just tired. We did a lot this weekend. What's up?" She stretched her arms over her head, took in a deep breath and exhaled slowly as she brought her arms down to her sides. "You must be excited. I heard you are booked solid for next weekend."

"Ella, I thought you were moving to Rhode Island. What changed your mind?"

She hadn't told him. *Grace!* But when? They were together all weekend. "Did Grace tell you?"

"No," he replied and took a step closer toward her. "Phillip told me Ava was the only one moving and that you were staying in Stratford."

"It's for the best." Her insides were trembling. She held back her tears as she thought about leaving Ava behind and returning to Connecticut alone.

"What about us? I thought we were getting along just fine."

She turned to face him. "I texted you, called you and you ignored me for the past two years and now you think?"

"Yes," he said and reached for her arm. "Ella, I was busy trying to get the inn open, you know that."

She nodded her head. "So ... now you have time for me?"

That hurt. David had no words, Ella was correct. He did give the inn all of his attention. "I'm sorry. I thought you understood how important the inn was to me. You were working, in Connecticut I might add.”

She looked across the street watching people run toward the ferry. Point Judith had a lot of foot traffic. She was glad they decided to open a second shop. She just wished she knew where his heart was and if he meant what he said the last time they kissed. She wanted to believe him, but something didn’t fell right. “What about Grace?”

“Ella!”

She turned to walk away. Took two steps, but stopped.

“Ella,” he said for a second time. “What about Grace? She moved out remember?”

“She stayed to be near you.”

“You’re wrong. Grace and I never had or ever will be in a relationship. I never looked at her the way I look at you. I knew the moment I saw you that I wanted to spend forever with you.” David was not about to beg her. If she wanted to stay in Connecticut, he would respect her decision and let her go. He started to walk back inside. Ella wasn’t the first woman to move on with her life and break his heart. The lighthouse caught his eye. “There’s room in my heart for you. I’m asking you to move to Rhode Island.”

Ella gently caressed his hand with her fingertips. “It’s a lot for me to consider. I have my apartment.”

“Rent it out. Move in with me.” He paused before saying, “If things don’t work out between us you still have your safe harbor.”

She laughed. "Are you always thinking about life near the ocean?"

"We make a great team. Give us a chance. That's all I'm asking. I promise you, I will give you my all."

From behind, they heard everyone coming outside. "Here," Ava said as she handed Ella her pocketbook. "I locked up. We're all going to Aunt Emily's for cake and ice cream."

"Crap!" David said. "I forgot his present at the house. Ella and I will meet you at Aunt Emily's." He looked at Ella waiting for her to respond. When she nodded, he knew he had one last shot to persuade her to move to Point Judith.

When they got in his Tahoe, David took her hand in his. "I'm asking you to move here because I want you in my life."

Ella looked out her window remembering last year. "I was here...the entire weekend for Hudson's first birthday and you never called me, asked to see me or returned my calls."

David turned off Route 108 and onto Route 1, knowing he had better tread lightly. Ella was correct, he knew she was staying at Grace's that weekend, but he had meetings with all the department heads and the inn needed him more than a one-year olds birthday party. "I'm sorry about that," he said and then let go of her hand to hold onto the steering wheel, he squeezed it so hard he thought he was going to rip it off. She had him in a corner. "I was needed at the inn."

"And nothing comes before your first love...right?"

From that moment on, David and Ella drove in their own silence until they saw Aunt Emily waving to them.

Ella smiled up at her. David waved back in return.

Before Ella got out of the vehicle she told David, "By the way, Hudson knew you were not there. He might have only turned one, but he knew. He kept asking for you. Oh wait, he saw you the next day when you took Grace to lunch." She got out of the car.

"What took you so long," Aunt Emily asked and then told them. "Everyone is waiting on the patio."

The backdrop on Aunt Emily's patio was decorated with a huge sign shouting, "Happy Birthday Hudson." There were yellow, light and dark blue Mylar balloons, fish, whales, yachts, and sailboats all with the number two on them. Next to the gift table was a big sign reading, "Ahoy! Our Little Mate is Two." Under the sign was David's gift a toy Tahoe for Hudson to ride around the yard in. David set his other present on the table next everyone else's. Aunt Emily had her gift––a large sandbox shaped like a sailboat delivered to Grace's house earlier that morning.

Grace watched as Hudson climbed in and immediately knew how to make it go. "Thank you," she told David and then told Hudson he had other presents to open. "Aunt Emily, Aunt Ella and Auntie Ava bought you a gift too." She pointed to the tricycle and told him to say thank you to everyone.

When Hudson ran to thank David, he saw Ella turn around to go in the house. A few minutes later, David found Ella sitting in the library drinking a glass of water. David sat down in the opposite chair. "Grace wasn't the only person I took to lunch that day."

Ella shook her head and rolled her eyes as if she didn't care.

"Ella," David said a little louder than he should have. "I'm sorry. I'd like to explain. If, you'll allow me to tell you what our luncheon was about."

Ella raised her glass. "Fine."

David leaned back, snapped his neck to the right and explained, "A woman on the beach asked if she could take a picture of Hudson building his sandcastle. After she explained she was a professional photographer on assignment for Rhode Island's Ocean and Coastal magazine—41DegreesNorth; Grace told her she could take his picture if she sent her a copy of the photo. They started talking and when she showed Grace the photos on her camera, Grace suggested she take pictures for the inn. I took the two of them to lunch and commissioned her to take scenic photos of Point Judith. As soon as the meeting was over everyone went on their way." He sat up in his chair ready to leave. "It was a business luncheon."

Ella pursed her lips before telling David she had a lot to think about.

Chapter Thirty-Six

Ella drove most of the way back to Connecticut in her own silence. Several times Ava tried to engage Ella in irrelevant conversation. She spoke about a new children's clothing line for toddlers, designing nautical sweaters for both shops and she spoke about Philip. "I think I'm going to break it off with Philip."

Ella continued driving without saying a word.

Ava knew Ella was thinking about something, but what? She looked at her wondering if she had second thoughts about opening the second shop. "Ella, are you having second thoughts about me running the new location?" Ava was still looking at her. Ella moved her left hand from the steering wheel, put her elbow on the driver's side door and rested her head in her hand.

Without looking at Ava, she said, "Not at all. I think you'll have a wonderful time." Then she took a deep breath, blew it out slowly and asked, "Why are you breaking it off with Philip?"

Ava would have a great time and who wouldn't? Point Judith was absolutely gorgeous and the tourism came from all over the world, but what she was asking was ... did Ella trust her to manage the new shop without her. "Our relationship isn't moving forward. We only attend big functions. We rarely have an intimate moment and I think he's seeing someone else."

"I'm sorry to hear that," Ella said and turned off the highway. When she pulled up to Ava's apartment, she told her she would see her tomorrow at the shop. "I'm really tired," she said and waved good night.

Ava reached back and grabbed her purse before asking Ella to open the trunk. "I need to get my bags out of the trunk."

"Sorry," she said and pressed the button to open the trunk. Ava got out, grab her bags and waved goodbye.

Ella drove away before Ava reached her front door. She was grateful to be alone. As soon as she reached her own apartment, she went inside, leaving her bags and her briefcase behind. She kicked a chair, tossed a magazine on the floor and collapsed on the couch. "Am I in love with him or just infatuated by him?" She sucked in a breath not knowing the real answer. An hour had gone by before she realized she didn't love David as much as she loved Grace and Hudson. They meant more to her than any man. "Hudson deserves a man in his life. Who better than David?"

She thought about Grace and her love for the man she lost. Ella prayed Grace would come around and eventually fall in love with David. "After all, David is perfect."

Ella's stomach plummeted, she felt sick. "Why?" She cried out. "Why did I kiss him? Why the hell does he have to be so damn good looking, charismatic and stable?"

Ella got up and went into the bathroom, turned the steam on in the shower, got undressed and sat down until she cried her last tear for what could have been her future. "I love you, Grace." Then she put on her robe, made herself a cup of tea and grabbed the book she started last weekend. At ten o'clock her cellphone rang. She picked it up and answered Ava's call. "Hey, is everything okay?"

"Would you mind if I didn't come to work tomorrow?"

"No, not at all," Ella said wondering if she was sick. "Are you not feeling well?"

"I have something important I have to take care of. I'll see you on Tuesday. Bye," Ava said into the phone and disconnected without waiting for Ella to respond.

The next day, Ava drove to Manhattan's Tribeca neighborhood. She grabbed the only parking spot available in front of Paisley—an Indian restaurant and walked to Phillip's apartment. When she reached 443 Greenwich Street, she asked the doorman if Phillip Jones was home.

"I'm sorry Ma'am, they left about an hour ago. Would you care to leave a message?"

"They?" Ava asked.

"Yes, he and his gentleman friend. I believe they said they were headed somewhere for breakfast."

Ava walked away feeling happy he wasn't with another woman. "Thank you, no need to tell him I was here, I'll call him in a little while."

Chapter Thirty-Seven

Two years after David purchased the old inn, a celebration was in order. Standing next to him at the ribbon cutting was Aunt Emily, Geraldine Prescott, Grace, her son Hudson, Ella, Ava and over two hundred fishing boat captains, mates and deckhands.

David made sure the invitation went out to the media in New York and all of New England, local magazines, restaurant owners and to every small business owner within a five-mile radius.

Six months before the grand opening, David's public relation person hired a florist, photographer, ordered gift baskets for every attendee, and started blasting on social media. The Lighthouse Inn of Galilee would be taking reservations starting that summer. She made sure at exactly six weeks before the event to send out a press release to the media, local newspapers and radio stations letting them know they were welcome to attend. Her office printed out maps of the inn showcasing every new and exciting detail. At the bottom was an invitation letting people know they could take a guided tour of the inn at two o'clock, along with a coupon offering a twenty-five percent discount on their first stay.

Next to the sign-in table was the first of many round tables filled with appetizers, and crafty desserts.

Under glittering lights soft music played in the background. And in honor of Aunt Emily's large donation to the swimming pool and its enclosure, signature martini's with silver lighthouses were tied to the bottom of each glass's stem. Beyond that a champagne fountain overflowed for guests to help themselves.

"No influencers or celebrities," David declared. "This inn is for men and women with families."

People brought unexpected gifts like snow globes with lighthouses in them. One person handed David a round large beautiful metal sign bearing the name of the inn under a lighthouse. "Thank you so much. This is very thoughtful of you," he said to the captain of Lil Toot Charters.

"This means a lot to us. I already have bookings into the fall thanks to you."

"Nothing makes me happier than hearing those words," David replied.

David felt a pair of large hands on his shoulders. When he turned around and saw Captain Andy from Misty Charters, he shook his hand. "Thank you for coming."

"I wanted to remind you about the firework display we are shooting off at dusk. I think you're going to enjoy it," he said.

"We're looking forward to it," David replied and then felt a tug on his pants. "Hey," he said and bent down to pick Hudson up. "Hudson these are real ship captains."

Hudson buried his face in David's shoulder.

Grace approached him from behind. "Sorry, I was at the kid's table, reached over to grab him a juice and he bolted for you."

"It's fine. Right, Captain Hudson? Grace, remember Captain Andy from Misty Charters?"

Andy held his hand out to her as Grace handed Hudson his juice box. "It's nice to see you again," she said as someone snapped a photo of the four of them. Grace waved to Melvin and his wife Jennifer as they entered. She wondered if it bothered Ella seeing him with someone else, but Ella assured her Jennifer was perfect for Melvin. She could get him to stop working in time for dinner and attend family events. Grace put her hand on Jennifer's belly. "Congratulations!"

"Hey," Ava said from behind. "David, Phillip and I wanted to give you this." She handed him an envelope.

David accepted it with one hand and shook Phillip's hand with the other. "It's nice to see you again."

Ella stood beside Grace. "Umm, are you ever coming in to see the store or what?" She said as she banged her hip into Grace's.

Grace laughed. "Yes, right now," she said and held her hands out for Hudson, but he was content being held by David. When he shook his head, she told him to be a good boy. Ella and Grace went arm in arm to see Ava and Ella's new store.

"I wanted you to see the finished product before we have our grand opening next Saturday," Ella said as she opened the door. "What do you think?"

"It looks fabulous," Grace said and closed the door. "Ella, please tell me Ava is wrong about you staying in Connecticut."

"I like living in Connecticut. I'm happy," she said as she pointed toward the new baby line of clothes.

When Grace read the sign, she smiled. "Hudson Line! Beautiful," she cried. Sailboats, tug boats, yachts and fishing poles were boasting everywhere. "Everything he loves."

"We expanded the play area so other children can play with him when he's here," she smiled adding, "for when he visits his Aunt Ava." Ella nodded her head. "She chose Point Judith. She'll run the Beach Store and I'll take care of the boutique."

"But, what about?"

"If she has any financial questions, David can answer them for her. I'm only a text away."

"Okay," Grace said dragging out the word. "I thought you were going to move here and let Olivia and Kayla run the Connecticut store? You said you were happy with them when you stayed with me last year. Why are you doing this to us?"

Ella snapped her neck back. "Me? You're the one who up and left. You can't expect *everyone* to stop living, pick up their lives and follow you to another state. Life doesn't work that way." Ella made a popping noise with her lips, crossed her arms and shook her head. "I'm sorry. You'll just have to trust me on this one."

Grace wore a puzzled look as her cell phone chimed. "Ava is wondering where we are. They're about to start the tour."

Ella offered Grace a weak smile.

"You seriously think she can manage without you?" Grace said as she turned to leave.

From behind she heard Ella lock the door. "She'll have you," she replied sounding as if she was about to cry.

Grace blinked several times as her own bottom lip quivered.

Ella stiffened as she entered the party. "I need a drink."

David waved to them as they approached the bar.

"Where's Hudson?" Grace asked as she accepted her dirty martini from the bartender.

"Aunt Emily has him. He's fine. She's taking him and Geraldine on a tour of the inn. She couldn't wait to show him the day care and all of the Little Tykes Toys."

Ella gave Grace a wry grin, turned toward David and said, "You put in a day care?"

"Yes, it was Aunt Emily's idea," David replied, handed her the Malibu Bay Breeze and then asked for a Michelob for himself.

Grace didn't know what to say. She knew Ella had her suspicions about her and David. "David wants the inn to be a family friendly place to stay. You'll see when you take the tour."

"Show her now," David said as he excused himself to greet Hugh Minor from Hey Rhody Magazine. "Hey, if it isn't the literary guru of New England. What do you think?" David shook Hugh's hand.

"You amazed all of us. Again! Seriously, your generosity to Point Judith is astonishing." He squeezed David's hand a little harder. "Congratulations!"

David told the bartender to give him another bloody mary. "Thank you, hey great article in Rhody Reads by the way," David said as he handed him his cocktail.

"Excuse me, can I get a picture of the two of you for the Narragansett Times?"

"Sure," David said and both men held up their drinks. David thanked the photographer and then asked him if he was sticking around for the tour. "Tour starts in a half hour."

"It's on my list of photos to take. You don't mind if I take a few shots of the bedrooms, do you?"

"Hell no," David said. "Take as many pictures as they will allow you."

"Thanks." The photographer said as he stepped away.

David turned to Hugh and asked, "So what are you up to these days?"

"Busy, I'm launching a new magazine, doing a little traveling. You know me, trying to spread kindness everywhere I go." Hugh looked past David. "I see Phillip found himself another trophy girlfriend."

David looked at Ava and Phillip, nodded their way and asked, "Him?"

Hugh blew out a breath. "Yeah, his rich family insists whenever he is in public that he be seen with the opposite sex."

David took a second look. "You mean to say?"

"Ever since he graduated from UCLA. He lives with his lover in Tribeca."

David didn't know what to do or think except, *poor Ava.*

"Excuse me, Mr. Wayne," his public relation person said to him. "I'd like to start the tour on time."

"Let's go," Hugh said as he and David followed her to the front of the room.

"Ladies and gentleman, may I have your attention," she called out. "Mr. Wayne would like to say a few words."

The room erupted in applause.

David searched for Aunt Emily and right before he was about to thank everyone, she appeared holding Hudson in her arms, sound asleep. He gave her a quick wave. "I want to thank everyone for coming here today. I could not have done this without the help of an amazing crew and a few women."

His assistant smiled at Aunt Emily, Ella and Grace knowing they all helped to make David's dream come true. She motioned for them to come forward, but they all shook their heads.

"Aunt Emily for believing in me and in my quest to save the inn. Grace for helping with the design, for all the late-night conversations and for being the friend I never knew I needed. And to Ella, for being so patient while I saw this project through."

Hugh raised his glass. "To the women behind the man, the myth, the legend!"

"Cheers," everyone called out.

David shook his head. "Please." Then he pointed to his crew gathered around the bar. "To the best damn group of men anywhere. I would work alongside you guys any time."

"Good," John hollered as he made his way toward David. "We got you a little something for your next project." John handed him a box, lifted the lid and put a white hard hat on David's head. "In case you decide to go roaming another construction site."

Everyone laughed, especially John's crew.

"Thank you," David said as he read the name printed on the front. "THE BOSS!"

The tour started with the gym, spa, dining room, conference rooms, banquet hall followed by the pool, David wanted everyone who was a resident of Point Judith to know they could buy day passes and swim in the pool all year long. "I hired a great life guard. The pool will be open from sun up to sun down, so please bring your little mermaids and merman." He laughed aloud adding, "You're never too young or old to learn to swim."

Then it was onto the guest rooms and the two suites. David stopped short and two women almost banged into him. "I'm sorry," he said to them. Turned around and asked his assistant to handout the flyers.

The women entered the room. One lady said, "I love it!"

Another person declared it was genius. "What a great idea," she said and asked if she could pull down one of the twin beds.

"Absolutely," David replied and held his hand out to her. From the other side of the glass people could see Grace's open floor plan. The woman was so impressed with all of the hidden storage areas, she called out to her husband. "Honey, there's even a place for your fishing gear."

That evening, everyone gathered near the pier to watch the fireworks. David had tears in his eyes when he read the aerial advertisement. The banner behind the aircraft read, "David Wayne. Your Fishing Family and Everyone in Point Judith, Thank You!"

Grace sighed, as she took it all in. The beautiful purple sky, sweet salt air, her son and the friends who refused to let go of her. She squeezed David's hand as she wiped away a single tear. He smiled at her and told her, "Thank you for helping me save the inn."

She kissed his cheek, looked into his eyes and replied, "Thank you...for saving me."

When the hospital settled out of court, Stefanie put all of the money into a trust fund for Hudson. In honor of Aunt Emily's large donation to the pool and its enclosure, David took all of the old stainless-steel appliances and opened a soup kitchen, "Auntie Em's".

As soon as the firework display ended, David hugged Ella and whispered in her ear, "Please choose Point Judith, it's the most beautiful place on earth."

ACKNOWLEDGMENTS

First and foremost, I must thank God for His many blessings upon me and my husband, for walking with us and for guiding my writing career.

Black Hawk Literary Agency, Jan Kardys and Barbara Ellis—the most caring literary agents in the business. Thank you both for being on my team.

To my family, friends, book friends, book club members, street team members and newsletter subscribers—thank you for believing in me and my stories. Most importantly, thank you for sharing my stories with your book loving friends.

Shout out to my beta readers: Pattie, Vickie, Lisa, Lynn, Joan, Tami, Carol, Corinne, Yvette, Betsy and Kathy your sharp eyes and feedback on clarity, plot, pacing, and grammar turned the manuscript into an unforgettable story. Blessing to all of you!

For information on how you can join my team email me at judyprescottmarshall@aol.com

Follow me on: TikTok ~ Judy Prescott Marshall

Facebook ~ Judy Prescott Marshall Author

Instagram ~ Judy Prescott Marshall

Goodreads ~ Judy Prescott Marshall

I encourage you to read one chapter *every* day!

If you are looking for motivation join my book club on Facebook.

bit.ly/Judy-Prescott-Marshalls-Book-Club

Thank you for reading my stories.
Buon appetite!
Ella's Malibu Bay Breeze
Malibu Coconut Run
Pineapple and cranberry juice over ice.
Garnish with a slice of fresh lime.

~

Aunt Emily's Blue Cheese Burgers
Start with a fresh toasted brioche roll.
Sirloin ground beef cooked to your desire.
Fresh spinach and a slice of tomato.
Topped with blue cheese.

~

Grace's Classic Lobster Roll
Start with a toasted buttered roll.
One pound of lobster meat.
3 Tablespoons of lemon juice, ¼ teaspoon of salt, 1/8 teaspoon of black pepper, ½ cup of celery finely chopped and 3

Tablespoons of butter. Sauté for three to four minutes. Add
lobster and serve immediately.

Do not overcook the lobster!

~

David Wayne's Linguine & Clam Sauce

Boil the pasta water and when ready drop the pasta in and cook
until al dente.

Chop two fresh cloves of garlic, one small onion, half of a red
pepper and six mushrooms. Sauté in ¼ cup of olive oil and one
stick of butter.

Steam the clams in one 8 ounce bottle of clam juice and a
Tablespoon of fresh parsley.

When clams open remove from shell and add to sauté pan
along with the clam juice.

~

ABOUT THE AUTHOR

Judy Prescott Marshall is an award-winning writer. She earned her certificate Write Your First Novel from Michigan State University. She is currently writing her next novel. She lives with her husband, David Wayne Marshall in Dutchess County, NY.

www.ingramcontent.com/pod-product-compliance
Lightning Source LLC
Chambersburg PA
CBHW050339030726
47503CB00008B/2523